Revealing the Shadows

A Detective Story

D.J. Maughan

Hulyeseg Publishing

For you, Brookey. You believe in me even when I don't believe in myself.
Your love and support means everything. I'll be forever grateful you said
yes.

Chapter One

Peter

December 25, 2000 - Budapest

Peter opens his eyes to find rich, chocolate-colored saucers staring back at him.

"Good morning." She says it without blinking, a slight upturn of her lips.

"Morning," he says, covering his mouth. "How long have you been awake?"

"I don't know."

Peter turns away, checking the alarm clock on the nightstand. It tells him what he already knows. He's slept too long and needs to hustle, or he'll be late for work.

Rather than get up, he turns back to her. Like always, the allure of being close to her pulls at him. Just a couple minutes and he'll get going. He hooks his arm under the pillow before putting his head back down. "You couldn't sleep?"

She shrugs, more of a slight lift of one shoulder. Her eyes never leave his. They lay on their sides, gazing at each other.

"I did, for a few hours."

This isn't like Karen. From the time they had first married, Peter was the one who had trouble sleeping. Early in his career, he found his sleep correlated to his stress level at work. Karen, on the other hand, rarely, if ever, let life impact her sleep. He would tease her that she could win sleep competitions if there were such things.

A pang of worry strikes him. Had he done something? Was he the reason she wasn't sleeping?

"Is something wrong?"

She doesn't immediately answer. She's aware of the words, but her eyes are distant. She's somewhere else. After a few moments, her gaze focuses back on him. "What are you investigating right now?"

It's not like her to avoid answering a question.

"Nothing, really, just a simple drug case."

Early in their marriage, he would tell her details of the cases he was working. But, as time has passed, he's intentionally been brief. Not because he has any reason not to trust her but because the case components were difficult for her to hear. She would worry and fret about his safety. He found the less she knew, the better.

"Why?"

There's that look again. What's going on in that beautiful mind?

She finally turns and lays the back of her head on her pillow, her chestnut hair cascading around her, framing her face. "I think I'm being followed."

Peter leans up on one elbow to look into her eyes. "Followed? What do you mean?"

She shakes her head, still looking at the ceiling. "I don't know...it's mostly just a feeling. A man walked through the nurse's station a few days ago. Nobody knew him. When another nurse asked him if he needed help, he said he was looking for a patient named Mitchell. We checked the logs and asked around, but we didn't have any patients named Mitchell. When we told him, he walked away. Never asking for confirmation. It was odd. Like he already knew." She turns her head to look into his eyes. "When I left work last night, I saw him in the parking lot. Watching me."

"Really? Where?"

"Sitting in a car. When I looked at him, he looked down and wouldn't look up. I think I surprised him."

Peter frowns. "You've never seen the guy before?"

She shakes her head.

"Kare bear...seeing a guy twice in the same location doesn't mean he was following you. For all you know, he double-checked the name and found the person."

"I know. But it was more than that. Something felt wrong about him. He scared me. I decided to get a taxi home rather than ride the subway. He gave me the willies."

"When you got here, did you notice him? Had he followed you?"

"No."

Peter smiles. "I hate to tell you this, but every man looks at you. You just don't always notice. You caught him checking you out, and he was embarrassed. I know I can't look away whenever I look at you. He probably saw you in the hospital and couldn't get you out of his mind. When he saw you in the parking lot, he admired you until you caught him. Any man would do the same."

She laughs, picking up his pillow and hitting him with it. "Shut up. I'm serious."

"So am I. I can't blame him. I'm not even mad. I'd do the same thing if I were him."

She sits up and presses her lips to his, wrapping her arms around his neck. He lets her push him back down to the mattress. He loves the feel of her body on his. After a long kiss, she pulls away and looks into his eyes.

"Let's be truant today."

"What?"

She slides her hand under his T-shirt and places it on his chest. "Let's stay home. Spend the day together."

Peter chuckles, looking back into her eyes.

"I'm serious."

And he knows she is. Not a hint of a smile plays on her face. *Why does she have to do this today?* Yesterday, he caught a break in the case he's investigating. A murder had been committed, and ballistics showed the murder weapon was a gun owned by a cop. The cop was put on leave while Internal Affairs investigated him, and Peter worked on the murder case. The cop claimed the gun had been stolen, and he hadn't reported it, believing it wouldn't matter. Internal Affairs believed him and gave him a slap-on-the-wrist probation. That didn't sit right with him. After working several leads in the murder, Peter came up dry. He decided to turn his attention to the cop and began following him. After a few days, he caught a break. Peter witnessed a transaction that looked like a drug deal. The cop gave a rough-looking man a backpack and received a package in return. Peter knew he was close to breaking the case wide open. He believed the cop played a part in the murder, maybe even being the shooter. Today, he'd obtain a warrant for his and his wife's financial records. Judge Clayton, his favorite judge, would only be available this morning. He had to get moving.

"I can't. I have a judge waiting on me."

Karen pouts and slides her hand down his chest. "Come on. Let's spend the day together."

Peter would love to but knows he shouldn't.

"I can't. But listen, let's go somewhere this weekend. Maybe we could finally take that trip upstate. Leave Friday and head up to Niagara Falls."

She frowns as he pulls away and looks at the clock again. He leans down and kisses her. "I'm sorry, babe. I want to. I can't."

Peter is roused from this memory by footsteps coming down the hallway. He rolls over on the dirty mattress. Two days ago, when walking up to Zsuzsa's apartment, Detective Szabo had stepped out from beside the building and a couple uniformed officers had detained Peter, claiming he was under arrest for the murder of Detective Kovacs Lajos. Kovacs was the leader of the Human Trafficking Task Force of the Hungarian National Police and Peter's boss. Peter was there when Kovacs died, and now he was blamed for it. Peter and Kovacs had been engaged in a secret meeting on Margit Bridge when a vehicle veered off the road and jumped the curb pinning Kovacs to the railing and cutting him in two. His body and the car were later recovered at the bottom of the river—but not the driver. Before the accident, Szabo didn't like Peter and wasn't quiet about it. With Kovacs's death, Szabo was promoted to head of the task force.

Peter was arrested and still had no explanation from Szabo or anyone else. He had not seen a judge and had yet to be offered an attorney. He spent the two days alone. Feeling more like a convicted murderer than a suspect. But now, company was on the way.

The footsteps shuffle to a stop outside his cell as two guards stand on either side of another man. The man is not tall, maybe four inches shorter than Peter's six-two frame. But he's very muscular, especially in his shoulders and chest. He has a shaved head and dark beard, touched with the first signs of gray. One of the guards opens the cell gate, pushes the man inside, closes the gate, and locks it. The guards look at each other, chuckling as they walk away.

Peter stands and looks at the man.

The newcomer motions to the bunk beds. "The lower bunk is mine."

Peter shrugs. "Fine with me. I'll take the top bunk."

He shakes his head. "That's mine too." The man's goading him. "You can sleep on the floor."

Peter stands, eyeing him.

"Do you have a problem with that?" The muscular man closes the distance between them. Peter isn't sure if he's got a weapon, but his intentions are clear.

Peter spits in his eye. The man falls back a step, crying out in surprise. Peter brings his elbow forward, striking the man in the nose. Too many people hit with their hands. Hands are full of small bones that break easily. Plus, elbows are harder. Blood springs from the nose as Peter balls his fist and punches the man in the stomach. He drops to his knees in agony. Peter knows he needs to strike one more time to incapacitate the man. If he has a weapon, Peter may lose his life.

As the man kneels on the ground, doubled over, holding his face, Peter grabs his head and brings his knee forward, connecting with the man's nose. Peter feels the softness of cartilage breaking. A tooth drops from the man's mouth as blood begins to gush. He falls back in a heap, hitting the concrete floor. His eyes wobble but never close. Peter comes forward and presses his knee into the man's sternum. Blood pours from his nose and mouth. Peter pushes his fist into the man's chest, controlling his breathing capacity. He looks the man in the eye, waiting until he can focus.

"Who sent you?"

The man looks at him and says nothing; anger and hate are in his eyes. Peter presses his knee in harder glaring back at him. The man winces and mumbles something unintelligible. Peter lets off some pressure.

"I don't know." The man wheezes.

Again, Peter presses harder.

"A guard." He coughs.

Peter pulls back his knee. "What did he say?"

"He wanted me to mess you up. He said if I did, he'd hook me up."

"What kind of mess up? Why you?"

"Cause I volunteered. He asked a few of us. I heard you used to be a cop. I was hoping to kill you. I hate cops. But he wouldn't let me. He said to only beat you up. Not kill you, scare you."

Chapter Two

Zsusza

I exit the empty subway, walk up the stairs, and approach the large glass building. Written on the exterior in big, bold letters is Hungarian National Police. Before this week, I never would have imagined I would ever come here. Especially on Christmas Day.

Two nights ago, I came after watching Peter's arrest outside my apartment. I had to know more and knew they'd bring him here. A security guard stopped me when I walked through the big glass doors. He told me that I had to leave; visiting hours were over for the night. I wasn't about to accept that. After a couple minutes of arguing, he could see I wasn't going to leave quietly. Having no other choice, he told me to sit down and that somebody would come out and talk to me. I waited and waited. Thirty minutes later, a massive man came down the stairs. I recognized him as the guy who had arrested Peter.

"I'm Detective Szabo. You must be Zsuzsa?"

I was surprised when he knew my name, but I shouldn't have been. After all, I was working undercover in the club and was kidnapped. Peter and Kovacs had come to Ukraine to save me. All the cops must know that story.

"If you know I'm Zsuzsa, you must know why I'm here."

He looked at me like I was some kind of nuisance. Which only made me dig in my heels. He told me he could do nothing for me and that I would have to return tomorrow. I demanded to know why he had arrested Peter, but he wouldn't tell me. To appease me, he promised I could see Peter if I returned in two days.

So here I am. I enter the front doors, and a new security guard stops me. He's got his officer uniform on, and like most of them, it's too tight.

"I'm here to see Detective Szabo," I tell him.

He asks me to take off my jewelry and put my purse in a bin, then walk through a metal detector. It buzzes, and he asks me to spread my arms and legs while he waves a wand over my body. He and his partner let their eyes linger longer than necessary before he tells me I can sit down along a set of chairs by the wall. This time, Detective Szabo descends the stairs after only a few minutes.

"Zsuzsa, good to see you again."

He extends his hand, and I hesitate before taking it. I'm not surprised when it engulfs mine. What's even less surprising is it's moist. After shaking it I wipe my palm against my leg.

"Peter was involved in an altercation."

My eyes widen with surprise. Before I can ask, he holds up his hand.

"Don't worry. He's fine. It was the other guy who needed to be taken to the infirmary. Peter jacked him up pretty good."

"Where's Peter now?"

"He's in a cell by himself. I'll bring him to the greeting room. But it needs to be short. He's not supposed to be talking to anyone."

He tells me to follow him, and we walk through the interior glass doors. After crossing through a hallway and descending a flight of stairs, another group of guards stops us. Szabo shows them his credentials, and they wave us through. We go through another hallway when Szabo stops outside a door, knocks, opens it, and ushers me inside. It's a small, plain room. Utterly void of pictures or furniture. A chair, counter, and telephone are on my side of the glass partition. The other side is furnished the same way.

"Have a seat. I'll go get Peter."

I sit at the counter, cross my legs, and feel my leg bouncing up and down. After five minutes, the door on the other side of the glass wall opens, and Peter steps inside. What hair he has left is tousled. He looks like he hasn't slept in days; bags are under his bloodshot eyes. He's wearing the same clothes I saw him in when they arrested him. I can see dried blood on the front of his shirt. When he sees me, he smiles, and my heart flutters. I need to help him. I want him out of here.

He sits down and picks up the phone, and I pick up mine.

He looks at me through the glass. "*Szia.*"

I look at him and don't trust myself to speak. I put my hand to the glass. I wish I could touch him. "*Szia,*" I finally reply.

He smiles a crooked smile. "Sorry about our date. I tried to come."

I see the pain in his eyes, the hurt. I know he must be scared. I'm afraid too, and I'm not locked up.

"I know. Why did they arrest you?"

"They say I killed Kovacs. Or at least, that's why I'm here."

"That's ridiculous! How can they say that?"

He shakes his head and sighs. "I don't know. They haven't told me what evidence they have. Do you remember what you and Kata told me in the restaurant before you worked in the club? About Andras?"

I watch him closely and let my mind fade back. I remember he came to the restaurant and met with us. We talked about a few different things. Peter sees from my silence that I'm unsure.

"You told me you both knew he was working with someone." A light-bulb goes on in my head, and he sees it in my expression. "A girl went missing in Újpest at the same time you were taken to Ukraine. I knew something was different about her. But if I'm in here, I can't investigate."

Somebody's put him in here to prevent him from investigating. But who? He's not saying, and I don't think he wants me to ask. He's being careful.

There's a clicking noise in the phone, and I swear I hear something that sounds like breathing. Peter's eyes focus on the phone, then come back to me. When they do, his expression is changed. The warmth in his eyes has been replaced with frost. He's shaking his head.

"Zsuzsa, it was nice of you to come, but don't come again. I don't want to see you anymore."

The words cut through me. Is he serious? What did I do? His face is deadpan. Impassive. His tone is hard and mean.

"Peter?"

"I'm serious, Zsuzsa. I never felt anything for you. I love my wife and could never love anyone else. I used you. I knew about Andras and what he was doing and used you to get close to him. I used you again in the club. I don't have any more use for you now. Go away, and don't come back."

He stands and hangs up the phone. He's through the door before I can close my open mouth. I sit holding the phone. Too shocked to move. Alone in the empty room.

Chapter Three

Detective Szabo

The door opens, and Zsuzsa walks out. Her head's down, and with her hair covering, I can't see her face.

"I'll show you out," I tell her putting a hand on her shoulder.

I glance in her direction several times as we walk through the hallway, past the guard station, and up the stairs. Her head remains down, her face covered. Finally, as we reach the main level, she looks ahead, giving me a view of her eyes. Tears brim her eyelids. Why does she care for him so much? She's such a beautiful woman, and he's a lying idiot. She deserves better.

I open the door and usher her out to the lobby. She's walking as if she's in some kind of daze. Barely aware of her surroundings. She looks numb. I expected her to badger me for information. Instead, she says nothing. Almost as if she's resigned to Peter's fate. It gets me wondering, did he admit something to her? Does she know anything? Has their relationship changed?

"Are you okay?" I ask as we reach the exterior doors.

She doesn't respond. I wonder if she even hears me. She walks through the outside doors and disappears. I'm left to stand alone in the lobby, looking after her. Something happened, and I've got to know what it is. I walk back downstairs, back to where Peter is. I get the jail key, walk to his cell, and open the gate. He's lying on the bed, hands under his head, looking up at the bunk above.

"Hey, Peter. I want to talk to you."

He doesn't move.

"Hey! Can you hear me?"

He still doesn't react, and I'm losing patience. I kick the bed, and he finally looks at me.

"I want to talk to you."

He frowns but swings his legs off the bed and sits up, staring back at me.

"What happened with Zsuzsa?"

He shakes his head. He knows better than to talk, but I'm not playing games. Maybe if I act understanding, he'll open up.

"Did you say something you regret? Maybe something she didn't want to hear?"

He turns his head in my direction. His look is ice-cold.

"Hey, it's just us. Talk to me."

He frowns. "You want me to talk to the guy who threw me in jail? No offense, but you haven't been friendly toward me since I came on the task force. Now you've arrested me and sent someone here to rough me up. Can you deny that?"

I wonder how he knows. Did one of the guards talk?

"I told them to make sure you weren't seriously hurt. Just roughed up a bit."

He chuckles and looks away. "How'd that work out for you?"

I feel a flash of anger. "Let's be real here. A rough-up is far less than what you did to Kovacs. What were you doing on that bridge with him?"

He shakes his head, not making eye contact.

"Look, you can choose not to talk to me. But then you're never getting out. Toth wants you to burn for this. Maybe if you explain it to me, I can get your sentence reduced. You'll get out of here someday."

"You haven't even told me what I've been charged with. I haven't appeared before a judge."

"And you won't if Toth gets his way. Who's going to save you? He can do what he wants with you. So, tell me what happened. Why were you on the bridge with him?"

My words land, and he turns his head to look at me; his eyes are hard. "How could I have killed him? Just as you said, I was on the bridge with him. I wasn't driving the car. I could have died as easily as he did. For all we know, I was the target."

"Yeah, but you didn't. He died instead."

"What do you mean, *instead*?"

"Why does it seem like everywhere you are, someone dies? It's convenient that it's never you. Your wife, Andras, and Kovacs. Even Csaba, the club manager, you were there when he was found dead in his cell. You're there every time. You're the link." He scoffs and tells me I'm stupid. "Say what you want, but you can't argue with that."

"Yeah, I can."

"How? Enlighten me. Tell me how stupid I am."

He looks straight ahead, and the anger I saw before is replaced with sadness.

"My wife was the love of my life. I've never been so happy as to be married to her. She was murdered by someone who wanted to get rid of me. They knew by killing her, I'd stop investigating them. And they were right. I couldn't do what I did before. I couldn't even stay in New York City. Everywhere I went reminded me of what I had lost. That's why I came back to Hungary. I was searching for something to keep me going. A reason to live."

This is the same story I'd been told before. But not by him, by other people. Coming from him, it hits a little differently. He's a good actor.

"Yeah, but what about Andras?"

"What about him? I think it's fairly obvious he tried to kill me. Ask Zsolt, the undercover who was working for him. He planned to kill Kata and me before Zsolt stepped in and saved us. I was a dead man on that train; it was pure luck. Andras tripped coming for me and got obliterated by the oncoming train."

"Luck isn't a very good reason for me to believe you."

He turns and looks me in the eye. "You don't have to believe me. There was a file on my desk. A girl was taken in Újpest. All of these victims are either foreign or from the country. This girl was from right in Budapest. It doesn't make sense. Something is different about that case. Her mom never reported her missing. It was five days later when a classmate reported her. That's the key. Get to the bottom of that, and you'll see very clearly my innocence."

I rub my face. "That girl's just a runaway. The MO changed because it's unrelated to the traffickers."

Peter shakes his head. "Only one way to find out. Find the girl. Talk to the mother. You uncover that, and you'll see I'm right. You'll know who the mole is in the task force."

Chapter Four

Peter

Footsteps wake Peter. He's been in jail for four days and was only released once when Zsuzsa came. Since Szabo's visit, he's been entirely alone. All the other cells around him are empty. The silence is eerie. He can understand why people tend to lose their minds with prolonged silence.

"Andrassy," a guard calls. "Get up."

Peter swings his legs off the mattress and stands. Even if they've brought another brute to terrorize him, it would be better than the last couple days.

"How does a shower sound? I can smell you from here."

His voice is gruff, but his eyes dance with amusement. The guard's average size. Probably mid-forties. His hair is more silver than brown. He's clean-shaven. He has a tattoo of the Virgin Mary and baby Jesus on his right forearm.

Peter nods with gratitude.

The guard waves his hand, indicating Peter should come forward. He walks out of the cell, and the guard points down the hallway. Peter passes most of the cells in his section of the jail. All are empty. He reaches the outer doors and stops.

"Turn right," the guard commands.

Peter heads down another hallway, this one much narrower. Ultimately, it expands into a dressing room with several metal shower polls spread evenly throughout the space. Peter stops in the middle of the room and looks around. It's empty, only him and the guard.

"Strip down," the guard commands.

Peter turns and looks at him warily.

"Ah, stop being shy. Strip down, go over to one of the showers, and turn the water on. Nobody's going to touch you."

Peter complies, and once he's naked, he walks across the room to the nearest shower column. He turns the metal handle under one of the heads and jumps back in surprise. The water's arctic cold.

The guard laughs and throws a bar of soap at him as he wipes his eyes. "Don't expect it to warm up. Only one temperature on those things."

Peter lets the water run at his feet before finally amassing enough courage to step back in. The water strikes him like tiny pinpricks. His lungs collapse, and he has trouble breathing. He takes the largest breath he can muster and holds on. Once he's wet all over, he steps back out and begins lathering his body with the soap. When he's thoroughly cleaned himself, he steps back into the water. He rinses himself as fast as possible and shuts off the tap. It's the fastest shower he's ever taken.

As he stands naked in front of the guard, the guard throws him a hand towel. Peter holds it up and looks back at him.

"Sorry, that's as big as they come."

Well, at least I don't have much hair. If he did, the hand towel would be thoroughly wet when he reached his neck. As is, he makes it only to his chest before feeling like there's little point in continuing. But, hoping he's wrong, he wipes the rest of his body, ringing out the hand towel a couple times. Once finished, he looks back to the guard. The guard points to a wooden bench. A light-blue jail uniform sits folded on it. Peter walks over and dresses himself. A pair of socks sit on the bench also, and he puts them on too. Peter stands, feeling much better about himself, and the guard waves him through another doorway.

Inside the room, Peter sees two pairs of shoes.

"This isn't a shoe store. The pickings are slim. Choose the pair closest to your size. A word of advice: when in doubt, go too big rather than too small."

The pair he picks must be at least a size thirteen. They're a couple inches too big, and he can feel his foot slide around as he walks. The guard steps in front of him and indicates Peter should follow. The guard walks up to a closed door, turns around, and looks him in the eye.

"We're going to let you have a little company for breakfast today." He points at Peter. "But there's a condition. No talking to anyone. If someone talks to you, don't talk back. Got it?"

Peter nods, and the guard nods back. He turns and opens the big, heavy metal door, and a flood of noise enters the small closet they stand in. The cafeteria is loaded with a couple hundred bodies, primarily inmates and guards. The guard tells him to follow, and they enter the large room. The guard walks to the front of the line, commands several prisoners to step back, then points for Peter to get food. Peter picks out some scrambled eggs and yogurt, then follows the guard as he walks him to a solitary table and indicates Peter should sit.

For the next ten minutes, Peter eats while observing the other prisoners. The guard stands next to him, saying nothing. Peter wonders why he's been assigned a personal bodyguard. Eventually, another guard calls out to his guard and waves him over. Peter's protection looks at Peter and hesitates, then walks over to converse with his buddy. He's no longer paying attention to Peter. Peter sees another inmate stand from a nearby table and approach. He's a big man with tattoos covering every inch of his exposed skin. Before reaching Peter, he looks over his shoulder at the guards. Peter grips his spoon, preparing for a fight.

When the man reaches him, he leans forward and mumbles, barely opening his mouth when he talks. "You a cop?"

Peter shakes his head.

The man glares at him. "Don't lie to me, pig. You see those guys over there?" He inclines his head in their direction. "They've been waiting for you to join us. They have a special party planned, and I'd be surprised if you survived it."

Peter stares at the guy as he walks away. He turns back to his food and then looks in the direction of the table. Two prisoners are staring at him. One raises his finger to his neck and makes a throat-cutting motion, then they both smile and laugh to each other. The guard returns, seeing Peter is done eating. He commands him to pick up his plate and spoon and throw them away. Afterward, Peter follows him back the same way they had come. They pass through the shoe closet and dressing room and walk down the hall. But instead of turning left back to Peter's cell, they turn right. They continue down another hallway, and the guard stops in front of what looks like the same door he had entered to see Zsuzsa.

"Somebody's come to see you."

The guard opens the door and waves him in.

Peter looks at him questioningly but knows better than to say anything. He pushes past him into the empty room, wondering if he's entering a trap. The guard closes the door. Peter looks around the room, wondering what he can use as a weapon. The chair is the only possibility, but it's lightweight and will only do a little damage. *Maybe it's not an ambush; perhaps Zsuzsa came back.* The thought both excites and worries him. He'd love to see her but knows it would only endanger her. She wouldn't be that stupid. After a few minutes, he sits in the chair and nervously waits.

Eventually, the door on the opposite side of the glass opens, and a man enters. Peter can't help the dumbfounded look on his face as the man sits across from him and picks up the phone.

"Gary?" he asks after he picks up on his side.

His brother-in-law smiles back at him. "I told you leaving New York City was a bad idea. But I never thought you'd get yourself arrested."

Peter couldn't be more surprised to see him. "How? What are you doing here?"

"What do you think? Getting you out of jail."

"How...how did you know?"

Gary laughs. "Funny story, actually. I got this weird call from Hungary. I thought it was you. I recognized the country code. But it was this old Hungarian guy. He spoke pretty good English. Anyway, he said you two are friends, and you were in trouble. He thought I might be able to help. He told me you were in jail for a murder you didn't commit, and I jumped on a plane. He met me at the airport and brought me over."

Peter shakes his head, worried his brother-in-law has made a trip for nothing. "It's good to see you, Gary. And I appreciate you coming, but I'm afraid there isn't much hope left for me."

"I see sitting in jail for a few days hasn't changed you."

"What does that mean?"

"I mean, you still think you know everything. I always thought Karen was too hard on you when she said you were a know-it-all. But she was right."

Peter smirks. Gary had always been the brother he'd never had. He looks at him through the glass and feels a touch of sorrow. He and Karen had been close, and Peter rarely saw Gary when his wife wasn't present. It just makes him miss her again.

"I bet you didn't know one of my buddies from Colombia University is a bigwig with the State Department, did you?"

Peter shakes his head.

"And he's close with a native Hungarian US congressman. That congressman is heavily involved in Hungarian American relations. Hungary recently joined NATO and cares greatly about maintaining a friendly relationship with the United States. So, even though I'd like to claim credit for soon getting you out of here, it's mostly luck on your side." Gary's smiling on the other end of the glass as he watches the impact of his words hit Peter. "Don't worry, brother, you'll be out of here soon."

Chapter Five

Director Toth

I step out of the black Mercedes Benz S-Class, turn around, and offer my hand to Eszter. Not that it happens often, but my wife insists on attending any funeral services for my fallen police officers. Especially when I've been asked to give a speech. I grip her gloved hand, help her from the car, and look behind us. A throng of photographers and reporters have gathered on the steps of Saint Stephen's Basilica. Kovacs's wife, Nadia, is a devout Roman Catholic. She insisted the service be held here. Eszter wraps her arm through mine as we turn and walk up the steps toward the basilica. The parasite media surrounds and follows us.

As we reach the top of the steps, one reporter calls out, "Have you any leads on Detective Kovacs's death?" Another hurls at me, "Are more police in danger?" Those are easy to ignore. But it's the next one that gets under my skin. "Director, why are you letting Budapest become more dangerous?" I stop and turn, glaring at the originator. Seeing the look on my face, the little man takes a step back, cowering under my gaze. Eszter squeezes and pulls my bicep, looking into my eyes.

"Ignore them," she admonishes.

I exhale and continue walking toward the building. We enter the doors of the vast basilica. The warmth of the building full of hundreds of Kovacs's friends, family, and colleagues engulfs us. This basilica is the largest in

Budapest and equal in height to the Parliament Building further north. Both are the tallest buildings in Budapest. The basilica was named after the first king of Hungary, Stephen the First. The building still houses his hand inside an ancient reliquary. You can barely recognize it is a hand at this point. It's mostly a pile of bones.

Eszter and I walk down the aisle of benches toward the front altar. I recognize several prominent political figures and nod to them as we make our way to the front. We take our spot at the end of the first pew. After a few minutes, the coffin is wheeled in. Behind it is Kovacs's wife, Nadia, and daughter, Noemi. Nadia is pushing Noemi in her wheelchair. The whole congregation rises when they see them. Nadia positions Noemi at the head of the front aisle and sits beside her.

The rest of us follow suit. Nadia turns and surveys the crowd, her eyes falling on me. I can see she's been crying. Her eyes are red and puffy. She nods a greeting, and I incline my head to her, keeping my face stoic. She looks at my wife and forces a smile. Eszter leans across the bench and pats her hand as she clutches a tissue in her lap. Cardinal Erdő, the cardinal of Esztergom-Budapest, is presiding. He stands and walks to the altar. He welcomes us and then adds a few remarks about the Kovacs family. When he finishes, he motions to me, and I walk to the podium. I turn and face the crowd of people and take a deep breath.

"I've known Lajos for thirteen years. Before my current role as director of the National Police, I served as captain of the Law Enforcement division. In that role, I was responsible for tracking down and apprehending criminals throughout Hungary. I was often called out to assess and review criminal matters, including theft, violence, and murder. Being new to the role, I made a special effort to become familiar with our detectives and as many police officers as possible. One day, I received a phone call telling me a shooting had occurred in the large Jewish synagogue a few blocks from here.

"I rushed out of my office and went to the scene, fearing the worst. The synagogue was packed that day, and someone had decided to carry out an act of violence on the congregation. I prepared myself for a horrific situation as I drove to the scene. I knew hundreds of people could be dead, many more severely wounded. When I entered the building, I found it almost empty. Confused, I located a group of officers and asked them for an explanation. The lead man pointed at Officer Kovacs. He told me a story of profound bravery and courage. Lajos was a beat cop in Erzsébetváros, the seventh district of Budapest. That day, he was stationed outside the synagogue. A man walked past who caught his eye. He wore a long coat and a backpack. The attire struck Lajos as odd, given it was August.

"Lajos followed the man, and when he withdrew a rifle from his jacket, he was ready. Lajos snuck behind him and took him down before the man could fire more than a couple bullets. Once subdued, they found multiple automatic rifles, ammunition rounds, and explosive devices. Only one person was shot that day, and she survived. Officer Kovacs Lajos saved tens, if not hundreds, of people. Some of those people might be your friends and family members. I was so impressed with his actions and demeanor that I promoted him to detective. From that time forward, he performed his duties with honor. Eventually, I made him head of a task force. I will always be grateful I had the opportunity to know and serve with my friend Kovacs Lajos. My condolences go out to Nadia and Noemi. He loved them so much. My hope is that we can all be a little more like Kovacs Lajos. Let's follow his example and do our best in everything we are tasked with. Farewell, my friend."

I stop and lock eyes with Nadia. Tears stream down her face. I leave the podium and make my way to her. She stands, and we embrace.

Two hours after the burial, I walk through the doors of the National Police Headquarters. I'm a man on a mission, and I know exactly where I'm going. The guards sitting inside the doors on either side of the metal detectors stand as I walk in. They call out in unison, "Good day, sir." I barely look at them, ignoring the protocol I'd put in place to scan each visitor. I walk through the metal detector, not bothering to empty my pockets. The red alarm above the machine lights up, and a loud buzzing noise blares through the lobby. I ignore it and keep walking. Behind me a guard protests. I turn around, my look challenging them. He turns white, and the other guard shakes his head, looking down. I turn back around and stride forward, crossing the lobby in only a few steps.

I push the door open, head down the hallway, descend the stairs, and walk up to the jail gate. Two more guards see me coming and stand at attention.

"Open the gate," I command.

One guard fumbles with the key and slips it into the lock. The door swings open, and I walk through.

"Where's Andrassy Peter's cell?"

One of the guards reaches over, picks up a clipboard, and runs his finger down the list. "Cell five-fifteen, sir."

"Good, take me there."

He puts the clipboard away and walks in front of me. We go through the jail, down a corridor, and eventually, he stops. We get to a corner area of the prison. No other cells are occupied near 515. I find this strange but don't ask the jailer. I step up to the bars and look inside. Peter is lying on his bunk. It's a bunk bed, but he's alone in the cell.

"Leave us," I growl at the guard.

He looks at me, then backs away. I stare at Peter through the bars. He sits up, looks in my direction, then stands. He leans against the frame of the bunk bed and crosses his arms.

"You've got some powerful friends. I've just learned you're getting out of here. A release by the Hungarian president." We glare at each other. "I'm not going to let you go without this warning." I slow my speech annunciating each syllable. "Never come back. Do you hear me? Go to New York or wherever and stay there. Resume your life there. I don't care what you do. But should you ever get the idea that you want to come back to Hungary, remember this. Don't. Forget about it. If you ever step foot in this country again, you'll regret it. Stay away. Consider yourself warned."

I can see in his eyes he's gotten the message. I don't wait for a response. I turn on my heel and stalk away.

Chapter Six

Lili

"Why are you reading that?"

I look up from the newspaper to see my friend and colleague, Anna, looking down at me. Her chin's resting on the cubicle wall. "I thought you were supposed to be researching your next story. You aren't going to find it in there."

I roll my eyes. "When did you become my boss?"

"I'm not. I just want to see you keep your job. Sometimes, when you aren't annoying, I like you. Plus, I'll be the youngest person here if you get fired. Who would I talk to?"

She's right, I'm the youngest reporter with the station. We work for Duna Television. Starting in 1992, Duna Television began when communism left, and the country became a republic. It started small, broadcast only over satellite. But after a few years it became a twenty-four-hour news station. The equivalent of CNN in the United States. I was hired six months ago, fresh out of the university here in Budapest. The recruiter liked me from the start. At five foot eight with long blond hair and bright-blue eyes, I was precisely what they were looking for. Since being a kid, I've wanted to work in broadcasting. I've dreamed of delivering the news to everyone in the country. In school, I specialized in broadcasting and political science. I was young when the Berlin Wall came down. I saw firsthand how much that changed our country. Those are the types of stories I want to report. So much has shifted in Hungary in my lifetime, and I want to be involved in it. Working for Duna Television seems like the perfect opportunity.

But, after being hired by Duna Television, I quickly learned they had another role in mind for me. It wasn't as the hard-charging political correspondent I had always longed to be. Instead, they couldn't get past my blond hair and trim figure. I was assigned the role of "Shopping Queen." My job is to find and report on shopping deals across the city and occasionally across the country. The store pays the station money to advertise, and I'm the lucky one who visits and reports on a particular product they want to highlight. For example, the customer might be a furniture company. I might be asked to visit the store and compare the mattresses for quality, price, and comfort. I hate it. This isn't what I went to school for, and Anna knows after just six months on the job, I'm anxious to report on something that matters.

"Unless you're looking at the ads in the paper, there's no reason for you to be reading it."

I glare at her. "Just because I'm the 'Shopping Queen' doesn't mean I don't have a brain. I'm interested in it. What's wrong with that? Plus, why don't you mind your own business."

She laughs, and her head vanishes. I can hear the click-clack of her keyboard. She's back to typing on her computer.

I look down at the copy of *Magyar Hírlap* open on my desk. The front page features a picture of Ferenc Mádl, the recently elected president of Hungary, shaking hands with the Austrian president. They were meeting to discuss trade relations and border control.

As I continue to flip through the paper, the title of an article stops me. It reads, "Eltűnt egy lány a papáról." (A girl goes missing from Papá.)

It has been two weeks since Sandor Margit saw her daughter. Her sixteen-year-old girl, Liza, went to Budapest to sing in a choir concert at the National Theater. As the teens boarded a bus headed back home, teachers found Liza was missing. They telephoned her mother to find out if perhaps a family member had taken her after the concert. Margit assured them they had no family in Budapest. The teachers searched the area before calling the police. An investigation got underway but has seen no success. Nobody saw or heard anything from Liza since the performance.

This most recent disappearance highlights a growing trend in the capital city. Over the last year, multiple teenage girls, primarily from the country, have gone missing since visiting Budapest. When asked for more information, Lead Detective Szabo declined to comment.

I'm pulled from my reading by the shrill whine of my telephone. I pick up the receiver and place it to my ear.

"Lili?"

I recognize my boss's voice, Böröcz Atilla, station director.

"Yes?"

"There's a farmers' market in Szentendre. Why don't you go up there and see if you can find anything interesting. They just bought an advertising package with us to help promote the event. Go up there, interview the event director, and get footage of different offerings. Take Tibor with you."

Tibor is one of our more experienced cameramen. He's often assigned to me since I'm the junior reporter at the station. I guess they think I need a babysitter.

"Yes, sir. I'll leave soon."

"Leave now. It's only open until five."

I hear a dial tone and know he's hung up.

I look at the digital numbers on the bottom right-hand corner of the screen. He's right, I need to get going. Szentendre will take at least an hour to drive to, and it's already two-thirty. But I can't stop thinking about that article. I turn to my computer, bring up the search engine, and type in the newspaper's name. After a surprising amount of searching, I obtain a telephone number and dial. I explain to the receptionist who I am and who I want to talk to. She transfers me to the reporter's phone. It rings, but his answering machine picks up. I leave a message. "Yes, Béla, my name is Horvath Lili. I'm a reporter with Duna Television. I'd like to discuss your article about missing girls in Budapest. Your article intersects with a special report angle we're working up. Maybe we can collaborate. Please call me back."

I hang up the phone and jump as I see Anna looking over the cubicle wall again.

"What do you think you're doing?"

"What?"

"Don't give me that. You know what. You aren't paid to investigate missing girls."

I shrug. "Girls shop."

She frowns at me.

"Don't worry. I have to go find Tibor. I can't wait to find what shopping treasures are waiting for me up in Szentendre."

Chapter Seven

Peter

Peter puts his carry-on bag into the bin above his seat and takes his spot next to the window. His brother-in-law, Gary, does the same and sits down next to him. Gary's only an inch shorter than his own six-two frame, and the two of them sitting side by side makes for a comfy row. Peter buckles his seat belt and opens the screen of the window. He looks out at the runway of the Budapest airport, Ferihegy II. The airport, although much smaller than the ones he's used to in New York, is nice. It's new, having only been completed last year. Replacing the original Ferihegy International Airport.

"Do they speak English at all on this flight?" Gary asks.

Peter turns away from the window to look at him. "I'm sure they do. But don't worry, I'll translate for you."

Almost on cue, the pilot comes on over the loudspeaker. The flight is operated by Malev, the official airline of Hungary, so all announcements are in Hungarian. Peter sits and listens while Gary stares at him. When the pilot finishes his statement, Gary continues to watch him.

"You've been on a million airplanes before. You don't need me to tell you what he said."

"Yeah, but even on French or German flights, I can guess what the pilot is saying. This doesn't even sound like a language. I can't hear when one word ends and another begins."

Peter chuckles. "Yeah, I think I was lucky to be a native Hungarian and learn it first. English seems much easier."

"So?"

"So what?"

"So what did he say?"

Peter shrugs. "The flight will be just under twelve hours. He expects it to be pretty smooth from here to JFK. Oh, and they will do their best to make sure we're comfortable."

"That's all he said? It sounded like he was talking for five minutes."

Peter chuckles again. "Well, he said a few other things, but you've heard it all before. It's a Budapest-based crew; thanks for choosing Malev; blah, blah, blah."

Gary seems satisfied and leans back in the seat and closes his eyes.

Peter resumes looking out the window as the plane pulls away from the gate and heads onto the runway. Like many others, the airport is on the city's outskirts on the Pest side of the river. As they taxi down the runway and lift off, he can't help the conflicted feeling in the pit of his chest. He's happy to be out of jail and excited to be returning to New York City. But he has unfinished business in Budapest, and leaving feels almost like giving up. As the plane accelerates into the air and banks to the right, he has a panoramic view of Budapest. He can't help wondering if he'll ever come back.

"What are you thinking about?" Gary asks.

Peter glances at him but notices his eyes are still shut. "How do you know I'm thinking about something?"

Gary opens one eye but still keeps his head against the back of the chair. "Just because you've been in Budapest for a year doesn't mean I don't know you anymore."

Peter smiles, and Gary raises an eyebrow, still keeping one eye shut.

"So, let's have it. What are you thinking about?"

Peter shakes his head. "A bunch of things. But just now, I was wondering if I'll ever return."

Gary closes his eye. "You know the terms of your release. They let you out under the condition of leaving the country. You go back, and they'll arrest you again."

Peter turns to look back out the window.

"What?" Gary asks.

"Only if one person is in power."

"What?"

Peter turns back to him, and Gary frowns.

"There's one person who threw me in jail and wants me to leave."

"Who?"

"Director Toth, the head of the Hungarian National Police."

"Why does the guy have it out for you?"

"Because I know what he is. And he used me as a scapegoat."

"Is that how you got arrested?"

Peter sighs and looks back out the window. "Yep."

Gary leans forward and opens the other eye. "Tell me."

"Well...when I came back to Hungary, I was broken. You know why I left New York. Everywhere I went, I was reminded of Karen. I couldn't live there without her. Returning to Hungary, where I hadn't been since I was sixteen, was helpful. I no longer thought of Karen and her killer every second of every day. It became more like every other minute. I began working as a PI, handling more minor cases like theft, infidelity, fraud, stuff like that. Cases I could choose. One day, I get contacted by a woman who thinks her husband is cheating. It seems relatively straightforward. I started following the guy, thinking I might catch him with his lover, and that's that. Except this time, it was much more than that. He was a trafficker. He was luring and abducting foreign and sometimes rural young ladies, then selling them. I got into a couple hairy situations with him but was able to expose the truth. I had a friend with the National Police who helped me with the investigation. That friend was made head of a human-trafficking task force under the direction of Director Toth. Kovacs, my friend, offered me a job as a consultant."

Peter shrugs and looks back out the window.

"I really didn't want to join. After what happened to your sister, I didn't think I could handle it. But he begged me, and I knew he needed help. My conscience wouldn't let me not do it. I began working with them and quickly identified a mole in the ranks. The traffickers were always one step ahead of us. Someone was tipping them off. A friend of mine went undercover for us in a club and was abducted. We were lucky to get her back; she was almost killed. Kovacs and I stopped sharing information with the rest of the force. We were making progress. The most we had in weeks, then he was murdered, and I was arrested for his murder. Sitting in jail gave me a lot of time to think. I'm convinced Toth is behind it. I'm not sure why he's doing it. And now, with Kovacs dead and me in America, he's got what he wants. The new leader of the task force is a guy Toth can control. He's not the sharpest tool in the shed. Even if he means well, Toth will stay two steps ahead of him."

Gary's listening intently. Peter shakes his head and leans back in his chair.

"Things are going to get worse. It feels like Toth has won, leaving me sick inside."

Gary's staring at Peter, barely blinking, anger in his eyes. "Something has to be done. People have to be noticing?"

Peter shrugs. "He's a powerful man. And he can use his power to cover his tracks. Unfortunately, it's out of my hands now. But, all this might have one bright spot."

Gary raises an eyebrow. "What?"

"I've got a new perspective on Karen's case. There's something I missed. And now, going back to New York, I can investigate it again."

"What did you miss?"

Peter shakes his head. "When she died, I was broken. I still am. I miss her constantly. I was going through the motions, trusting my former colleagues to investigate her murder. I relied on them. I now realize that trust was misguided. Instead of trusting, I should have been investigating them."

Gary grabs his arm. "Are you saying the police killed Karen?"

Peter nods. "That's exactly what I'm saying. Now I just have to prove it."

Gary looks at Peter, his mind working. Finally, he sighs and leans back. "How are you going to do that?"

Peter shakes his head. "I'm not sure yet."

The flight attendant comes by and asks if they want anything to drink. Peter requests water and translates for Gary, telling her he wants a cola.

After she serves them, Gary leans back and sips on his drink, looking at the seat in front of him. "You said you had a friend abducted by the traffickers, a she. Are you dating her?"

Peter looks at him, sighs, and turns back to the window.

"Peter, I'm not going to be mad. I'm surprised but not mad. I think it's great. I think Karen would want that for you. She wouldn't want you to be alone."

Peter looks down and begins drawing the pattern of an eight, over and over on his trouser leg. Finally, he looks up.

"I met her in a bar while investigating the first trafficker. I wasn't looking for anyone, but I'll admit, I was drawn to her from the start. We went on one date and had another planned when I was arrested. I won't lie, I do have feelings for her. She came and visited me at the jail. Someone was listening to our conversation. Even though I didn't mean it, I told her I didn't care about her. That I never wanted to see her again. I did it to protect her. If

Toth thinks I care for her, she's in danger. For her own good, I can't contact her again. She thinks I'm still in jail."

Gary looks at Peter and shakes his head. Finally, he sighs and closes his eyes again. Peter turns back to look out the window. They're above the clouds now, and he closes the window screen. He leans his head back and shuts his eyes, hoping he'll get at least a couple hours of sleep. He told Gary he feels regret about not stopping the trafficking in the city. And that's true. What he didn't mention is the more significant regret. Another woman he cares for has been taken from his life, and he feels powerless to do anything about it.

Chapter Eight

Zsuzsa

I walk into the restaurant, and I'm greeted by the new hostess.

"Hi, Zsuzsa."

I don't remember her name. Marta, maybe? Kata hired her while I was in Ukraine, and I've only worked with her once. She's young and cute, like most of them. She wears her dark-brown hair short and has a sleek, dark-green dress with high heels.

"Hi," I respond as I hang my coat. "How have things been today?"

She smiles a bright smile. She has straight, white teeth and full lips. Her lipstick is bright. "A little slower than usual. Maybe that means tonight will be popping."

Her enthusiasm makes me smile as I walk toward the office. A few days ago, Kata and I had decided to take turns managing the restaurant. After Andras was killed, she became the owner and took to it like she was born to do it. The atmosphere is so much more inviting for all the employees. Having never worked in a restaurant before, she's leaned on me for help and support and promoted me to manager. Now we take turns. She'll work the days, and I'll work the nights or vice versa. Today, she worked the day, and I've got the night shift.

I greet a few other employees on my way to the office. I enter and find Kata sitting behind the desk. Her head's down, and she hasn't noticed me yet. I clear my throat, not wanting to startle her but also to alert her to my presence. She looks up.

"Oh, Zsuzsa. Is it that time already?" She looks at her watch.

"How's it going today?"

She stands from the desk and comes forward. We go through our typical greeting, kissing each other on both cheeks starting from the left. She heads back to her chair behind the desk, and I sit on the side.

"It's been a little slower than I'd hoped. I was thinking maybe we should put some money toward advertising. What do you think?"

"Might be a good idea. What kinds of ads?"

She shrugs. "I'm not sure. I wish I had more of a business sense."

I absently push an invoice back and forth on the desk. "I had a thought. Maybe we should try something on the internet. It seems like an emerging method. I don't know much about it yet, but I could do some research. I've seen other restaurants doing it."

She looks at me in wonder. "You're a lifesaver, Zsuzsa. Where would I be without you?"

I wave my hand. "It's fun, isn't it? I love the challenge."

"It is, but I wish I knew more. I've never really done much with computers, but Andras had one at home, and I've started playing around on it. I'm thinking about maybe taking a class." She frowns. "There's just so much to learn. Because of employees like you, the restaurant feels like it's gone pretty well." She smiles. "You might not agree."

I reach over and put my hand on her shoulder. "You've done great. I'm so impressed."

She beams and tells me I'm sweet. Then she shakes her head. "It's the business side that's so hard. Knowing how much food to order and when. How to advertise and get more people through the door. But also not waste the money. It's not like I have tons. I also have a hard time knowing when to change our prices. I've kept them the same since Andras." She throws her hands up in the air. "It's kind of overwhelming."

I stand and wrap my arm over her shoulder giving her a squeeze. "How can I help? I'm happy to do more."

She reaches up and pats my hand. "You already do so much, managing the employees and working out the schedules. I couldn't do it without you."

I squeeze her shoulder. "I'll do some advertising research. See what I can learn. We're in this together."

She stands and gives me a hug, then steps back. "Now, on to more important things; what's going on with Peter?"

I knew she was going to ask, and I can't meet her gaze. A pencil sits on the desk, and I push it around with my finger. "I went and saw him at the jail."

"And?"

"He told me not to come back. He said he never really cared for me and doesn't want me to visit anymore."

"What? You're kidding."

"I'm not."

She puts her hand on my shoulder.

"The thing is, I could see in his eyes he was lying. When he came into the room and saw me, I could tell how excited he was. He wanted me there. At first, in the conversation, he was sweet. But then something changed. I think he heard something. I don't know. I think he told me not to come back to protect me." I look up at her and shake my head. "I think about him all the time. What's going to happen to him?"

"You don't think he's guilty, do you?"

I shake my head. "No way. Do you?"

"Of course not. He's being set up."

"Before he told me not to come back, he mentioned another girl. A girl in Újpest went missing, and her mother never reported her. He said he was investigating that when he got arrested. He said she was the key to this whole thing. I'm going to see what I can find out about her. Maybe that's how I can get him out of jail."

"Hun…be careful. I don't want to see you get abducted again. Peter won't be around to save you."

"I can't just leave him in there. He needs my help."

"Agreed. But that doesn't mean you need to be the one investigating. Maybe you can find someone else to do it. Maybe I can help? I hired Peter, remember? Maybe there's a private investigator out there somewhere. Someone we could contact."

I hadn't thought about that, and I shrug. Still, private investigators cost money, and I don't have much. I doubt she does either, given what's happened to her lately.

"I wish we could trust the police," she says as if reading my thoughts.

"Me too. Well, I should probably get out there. It sounds like it's getting busier."

As I walk to the office door, she calls my name, and I turn around.

"Promise me you won't start investigating this girl on your own, okay?"

I nod and head out the door. The dining area is getting busier. Multiple tables are occupied, and the bar has the most seats filled. I go over and help tonight's bartender, Csaba.

After that, I help in the kitchen, dining room, and bar for the next few hours. Most of my time is spent at the bar. I just seem to gravitate to it. I'm comfortable there. I guess it's years of bartending. At times I miss it. I like managing. I like the variety of it. But at the bar, I'm home. I talk and flirt with my regulars. I always did really well with tips, and now, as a manager, my salary is better, but my tips are much less. I miss walking out at the end of the night with a bunch of cash in my purse.

Our hostess goes on break, and I take over for her. I stand at the front of the restaurant, looking over the dining hall as I wait for someone to come in. Two couples, one right after another, finish their meals and leave. I greet them with a smile and wave as they pass, wishing them a pleasant evening. As the last one walks out the door, a man enters. He's pretty tall, maybe six foot. He has wavy, light-brown hair parted on the side. He's wearing a sweater and coat, but I can see he takes care of himself. His shoulders are broad, and his waist is narrow. He has the stereotypical V shape. As he comes in the door, he looks at me, and I feel my face fill with color.

It's not just because of his defined jaw and piercing blue eyes. I know him somehow. But I can't place it.

"Hello," he says as he stands in front of me.

I look up at him, but for the life of me, I can't find something to say.

"I thought I might get something for dinner."

He's smiling at me, and I melt. He has such a nice mouth and white teeth.

I pull myself together and ask, "Table for two?" He's too good-looking to be here alone.

He shakes his head. "No, it's just me tonight."

I nod, and that knowledge excites me. My cheeks are hot, and I look down, groping for a menu. As I turn back to him, I look at his hand and notice no ring.

"I can show you to a table."

"Actually, I was hoping to sit at the bar."

"Oh...sure. Follow me." I turn and walk in front of him, now mindful of how I might look from behind. I reach the bar and turn back to him, pointing to a stool. "How's this?"

He smiles that delicious smile and nods. He wears a scarf loosely around his neck and a long overcoat.

"Do you have somewhere I can hang my coat?"

"Sure."

He unbuttons his coat, reaches his arm through one sleeve, then works it off, swinging it back around. His sweater is tight across his chest and shoulders, and I can't help admiring the view. He hands me his coat, and I'm surprised by the weight of it. It's heavy.

"The bartender will be with you in just a moment."

I walk toward the closet in the back hall and smell the scent of him as I hang the coat. There's a faint smell of cologne, and I fight the urge to bring it closer to my nose. My cheeks still feel hot. *Zsuzsa, get it together. You've seen handsome men before.* But there's something different about him, something familiar. I can't place it. But I know him.

After hanging the coat, I return to my post at the front of the restaurant, occasionally stealing glances at him. After five minutes, the hostess returns, and I'm free to roam the restaurant. I greet customers, help where I can, and serve a few drinks at the bar. Always conscious of him but never making eye contact. Finally, after an hour, one of my regulars calls me over. We chitchat, and he's flirting with me, but I don't flirt back in the usual way.

"What's wrong with you, Zsuzsa? Are you okay?"

I smile and touch his shoulder. "I'm sorry, just a little tired tonight."

I look up and see the handsome guy watching us.

Csaba, the bartender, asks if I can help out for a minute and leaves. I come around the bar and feel the man's eyes on me. He's still watching me. I look up, and he smiles.

"Your name is Zsuzsa?"

I nod and move to the opposite side of the counter.

"What's your family name?"

"Why?"

"Is it Másik?"

This takes me by surprise, and I frown. *Who is he? What does he want?*

"I think we know each other. You were friends with my sister. Did you grow up in Érd?"

As he says it, it clicks like a thunderbolt.

"You're Gábor, aren't you?"

He laughs. "I haven't seen you in forever. How are you?"

I can feel myself smiling so big I might split my lips. "I'm doing great! How are you?"

For the next five minutes, we catch up. He was my best friend's older brother, and I always had a crush on him. He was four years older and never seemed to notice me.

"So, are you the manager here?" he asks.

"I am. I've worked here for six years. I used to tend bar and just recently got promoted."

He nods. "Married? Boyfriend? Kids?"

I shake my head and think about Peter, feeling a little guilty. He's not my boyfriend. I care for him. But we've been on one date. That's hardly boyfriend material.

"What about you?" I ask.

"No boyfriend for me," he says and chuckles.

I shoot him a look, and he laughs again.

"I'm divorced. I have a son, he's eight. I don't get to see him as much as I'd like." He picks up his beer and takes a drink.

"What do you do for work?"

"I work for an advertising firm."

"Really? Know anything about advertising for a restaurant?"

He purses his lips and nods. "Plenty. Do you need some help in that area?"

I shrug and hear Margit, the chef, call me from the kitchen. "I've got to go," I tell him, not wanting to leave.

When I come out of the kitchen ten minutes later, he's still sitting there. He's done with his beer and food. Csaba gives me a look and inclines his head toward him. I look at him and walk back to Gábor.

"I've got to go. But I have a question for you."

I have a pretty good idea what he's going to ask and can't help my internal battle.

"Can I take you to dinner on Friday night?"

I hesitate, and he sees it.

"Free dinner and…you can ask me anything you want about advertising."

I smile but still hesitate.

"Come on. It's just dinner."

"Okay."

He smiles, and I get his coat, then walk him to the front door. He asks for my number, and I give it to him, and he writes it down. We say goodbye, and he walks out.

The hostess is back at her post.

"Wow! He's gorgeous, isn't he?"

I turn and look at her. "He is."

"Do you know him?"

"I grew up with him."

She smiles. "Make sure he comes back. He's fun to look at."

I smile and walk back to the office. I sit down at the desk and start reviewing the shift schedule for the weekend, but I can't concentrate. I can't help thinking about Peter in that jail cell while I go to dinner with another man. I chastise myself for saying yes. Peter needs me, and I'm moving on to other men.

Chapter Nine

Detective Szabo

I never realized all the bureaucratic nonsense Kovacs had to deal with. Now, as head of the task force, it falls on me. Half my time is spent answering to others, especially Toth. Before, I would see him here and there, and he was always so pleasant. Now, he's constantly breathing down my neck for information. Every day I have to file a report with him. He wants to know what we're working on, along with any new developments in the human-trafficking syndicate. It's almost like he cares about nothing else. I wonder if the other taskforce and department heads also deal with this. How could he have time to read every report? At least now he lets me send it as an email. Kovacs used to type it up daily and deliver it in person. I never truly appreciated all that Kovacs had to deal with.

After I hit send, I hear a knock at my door.

"Come in."

The door opens, and Rákosi Gyula, head of the major-crimes unit, stands in the doorframe. He's a small man, not what you would expect for someone who leads a team of investigators who track down killers. He's maybe five foot six and weighs less than one hundred and fifty pounds. What he lacks in physical stature, he makes up for in personality. He's the walking definition of the Napoleonic complex.

"Szabo, don't you check your messages?" He glares at me, but I have no idea what he's talking about. I glance down at my phone and see a red-light flashing. I could swear it wasn't doing that when I came in this morning.

"Sorry, Gyula. I didn't notice it. Toth has been all over me about his daily report."

"Yeah, cry me a river. We all have to report to him. Get used to it. That doesn't mean you drop everything else. You have a job to do."

I feel my blood pressure rise and fight to control my voice. "Like I said, I'm sorry. I didn't see the message."

He waves a hand. "Well, if you had heard it, you'd know I'm looking for a file. A young girl has been found in a dumpster in Újpest. We think it might be a girl who went missing a couple weeks ago. The log says it was last checked out to Detective Varga. Out of respect, I wanted to talk to you, department head to department head, before asking her about it."

"Thank you. Let's go ask her."

I stand from my desk and walk with him to the bullpen of cubicles. Varga sits at her desk, reading something on her computer.

"Hi, Varga. Gyula's looking for a file." I turn and look at him, realizing I never got the missing person's name.

He looks down at the paper he's carrying. "Name of the girl is Sándor, Judit."

Varga has several files on her desk and starts rifling through them. Finally, she shakes her head. "I don't have a Sándor..." She stops, her eyes darting over to Peter's old desk. She stands and brushes past us. She shuffles through files on the desk. "Here it is." She holds it up, then hands it to Gyula.

He thanks her and moves to leave.

A realization dawns on me. After talking with Peter in the jail cell, I never researched the missing girl he'd referenced. He said the file was on his desk.

He was sure it would lead me to the mole. Could this be the file? Had the girl been found?

"Gyula?" I call out, catching up to him. He turns around and looks at me. "You say her body might have been found in a dumpster?"

"Yeah, apparently it's a pretty nasty scene. I'm headed there now."

"Mind if I come along?"

He shrugs and starts walking. I follow.

Twenty minutes later, we pull up to the address in Újpest. It's impossible to miss. There are four police cars and yellow caution tape creating a perimeter. Several curious bystanders stand outside the tape, pointing and whispering to each other.

Gyula walks up to the tape, and one of the detectives pulls it back for him. He has to raise the tape for me, and when he does, he eyes me strangely. I've seen the guy a few times but don't know his name. He's tall, probably about my height but at least fifty pounds lighter and ten years younger. He's clean-shaven with dark-brown hair and brown eyes. He's got a funny-shaped nose that looks like a parrot's beak.

"Detective Csonka, this is Detective Szabo. Szabo, Csonka," Gyula says without looking at either of us. His eyes are forward, focused on the green dumpster. "Szabo is head of the trafficking task force." He looks at Csonka, seemingly waiting for him to speak.

Csonka stares down at him as Gyula's look goes from stern to crusty. "Oh...right. Well, we got a call from this cleaning woman over here." Csonka points to a woman standing next to one of the police cars. She's young, maybe late twenties. She's clearly got gypsy blood in her. She has dark-brown or maybe black hair pulled into a ponytail. Her skin is also dark. She's average height with a runner's build.

Gyula turns in her direction and walks up to her. He extends his hand, smiling. "Ma'am, I'm Detective Rákosi. Thank you for calling us."

She takes his hand and nods. She looks down at her feet.

"Do you work nearby?" Gyula asks. I barely recognize the voice. I've never seen him like this. If you could see his words, they'd be dripping with honey. She doesn't look up but nods. "We'll get you out of here as soon as we can. Do you mind if I ask you a few questions?"

The woman looks at me and Csonka, then back at Gyula before shrugging.

"What made you call us? What did you see?"

Her eyes dart over to the dumpster, then she looks back at the ground. She's holding her hands in front of her, and her pinkie finger is twitching. "I clean the building next door." She looks up and points to the building across the alley. "I was just finishing up and taking the garbage out. I had a lot. I was sick for a few days last week, and with Christmas...there was a lot. I had a garbage sack in each hand. I put one of them down and reached for the lid. That's when I saw it." She puts a hand to her mouth. Tears roll down her cheeks.

Gyula waits a beat before asking, "What did you see?"

She shakes her head, and her eyes dart back to the dumpster. "There was blood on the lid."

"How'd you know it was blood?"

She raises her gaze to look at him. Lightning flashes in her eyes. "I'm a cleaning woman. I see blood. Sometimes a lot of blood. I know what it looks like."

Gyula raises his hands. "I didn't mean any offense. Just wondering how you could tell."

She looks back down, and her voice is calm again. "The color. And the consistency of it. There wasn't a lot, but when you see the dumpster almost every day like I do, you notice something like that. Something out of the ordinary."

Gyula nods.

She looks back at me, and our eyes lock. She begins talking to me. "I opened the lid, a little afraid of what might be in there. I looked inside and saw nothing but bags of trash. The can was half full. I was relieved and reached for one of my bags, but as I swung it up into the dumpster, I noticed more blood on one of the trash bags."

Gyula raises a hand. "This was a sack in the dumpster? Or the one in your hand?"

"One in the dumpster."

Gyula nods and motions for her to go on.

"A few months back, there were some cats that went missing. One was found in the dumpster. Mutilated. I was thinking it would be something like that." She shudders and looks away again. "It wasn't." She looks back to the dumpster and points. "I got that stick right there and started moving sacks around. That's when I saw her." A tear rolls down her cheek, and she reaches up to wipe it with her palm. She hugs herself, and for the first time, I feel the cold. "Her eyes were open, blood everywhere. She was gray. I've never seen a dead body before. But I knew she was dead."

Gyula nods and waits. When it's clear she's not going to say anything else, he asks, "Did you know her?"

She bobs her head. "I don't know her name. But she lives in the building I clean. I've seen her a few times."

"Do you know which apartment?"

After getting the apartment number and her contact information, we let the woman go and move to the dumpster. A box has been placed at the side. Neither Csonka nor I say anything, but we both know who the box is for. It's not for either of us. I can feel my heart pumping a little harder as I approach. I'm not sure what I'm going to see, and no matter how many dead bodies you've seen, it's still not something that's easy to deal with.

The three of us make eye contact before looking in. Bags are stacked up along the sides. In the middle, a dead, bloated body lies along the bottom of the dumpster. She's young. You can tell that right away. Probably fourteen or fifteen. Blood, the color of tar, surrounds her with patches over her clothes and skin. A large gash extends along her neck. It's a dark, dried-blood color now. It looks like a giant spider arm.

But it's her eyes that are the most eerie. I don't think I'll ever forget those eyes. They're hollow and lifeless and staring right at me. It's like they're trying to speak. But I'm not sure who's delivering the message. Is it the girl? Or is it the murderer? Did the murderer intentionally set the body so the eyes would stare at us when it was found? I step back from the dumpster and take a few deep breaths hoping I don't pass out.

Chapter Ten

Peter

After exiting the subway, Peter walks a half mile to the bus stop, riding it until Union Turnpike before exiting. He then walks a quarter mile before reaching the wrought iron fence that surrounds the cemetery. To this day, he's never spent much time in Queens. He's only ever been to this graveyard once, fourteen months ago. It's a day he'll never forget. He reaches the front entrance and walks through the gates. Everything looks the same as that day. A seemingly endless number of headstones packed as if on top of each other. The trees are bare, the grass is brown and dormant, and no birds are singing. In another month or so, buds will pop out on the tree branches. But for now, everything looks dead.

The weather on the day of the burial was unseasonably warm. Not a cloud in the sky. Peter remembers thinking how ironic it was. A black cloud hung over him while the sun shone. As he walks along the path, he finds the weather today to be more appropriate. It's cold and overcast, threatening snow. Approaching the reason for his visit, he feels lightheaded and realizes he's holding his breath. Whenever he's anxious, he does this. He releases the air in his lungs and sees it float away. He sucks in a large quantity of crisp oxygen and reminds himself to breathe. Grave markers litter the brown grass as he walks between them.

He and Karen had never discussed where they might be buried. The thought never crossed their minds. That was always a discussion for much older people. Little did they know she would leave this life so early. Peter can remember sitting in his living room with Gary and Becky just days after Karen's murder. The funeral director sat before them, reviewing a checklist of items to be done. Peter felt numb answering each question but was able to stumble through most. When the question of where Karen should be buried came up, he was stumped. After seeing his hesitation, Gary jumped in to help. He suggested Peter consider the Flushing Cemetery in Queens. He said several family members were buried there. Peter agreed, and here he is. This is his first time back since they lowered Karen's coffin into the ground.

After that fateful day, Peter told himself he would return. But he couldn't bring himself to come back. That day, as he looked at her coffin, he couldn't feel her presence. He felt cold and lonely. The cemetery itself felt stiff and lifeless. Everything about it was wrong for Karen. She was always so warm and full of life. He didn't want to picture her there and found himself making excuses not to return. Guilt would overtake him at times, knowing that it's expected for loved ones to visit. But the thought of being there, seeing her headstone, was too much. Those words in stone were too final, and he couldn't bring himself to see them.

Then he left for Hungary and couldn't visit even if he wanted to. He told himself if he ever came back to New York, he'd force himself to return. Now he's here. He's reached the spot under the elm tree. He stops walking and closes his eyes. He knows he's standing right in front of her grave marker, but he hesitates. He takes a big breath and opens his eyes. The gravestone is light gray with black block writing. He's been expecting the pain that would come from seeing those letters. The finality. But it's even worse than expected. Below her name is her birth and death dates. He finds it hard to breathe as tears spring to his eyes.

After staring at the stone for minutes, he walks around to the back. He's surprised to see there's a quotation there. It's a line from a poem. He can't remember picking this out. Gary and Becky probably took care of it.

Since There's No Help, Come Let Us Kiss and Part.

The sting that comes with those words leaves him feeling numb.

No Help.

Is that what Karen felt? Was she helpless? She had tried to tell him she was in danger, and he had ignored her. Passed it off like it was some harmless flirtation. He had lost the most vital thing in his life because of his ineptitude.

As he stands, staring at those words, he feels a resolve build within him. He lost Karen because of his own carelessness. But he isn't going to allow her killers to go free. If it means losing his own life in the process, they will pay for what they did to her. He owes her that.

Chapter Eleven

Director Toth

I hear a knock at the door as I stand looking out the floor-to-ceiling window of my office.

"Come in."

I look in the direction of the door. It opens, and in walks my childhood best friend, Németh László, the mayor of Újpest. He shuts the door behind him and walks over, sitting on the other side of the desk. My gaze returns to the city below.

"What brings you to police headquarters today, Mr. Mayor?" I look down at the traffic jam of cars, waiting for him to speak. But he doesn't. Finally, I turn around and look at him. He's sitting at the edge of the seat. His hands are on his knees, his gaze focused on the desk. I turn and walk toward him. "Laci, what is it?"

Finally, he looks up at me. His face is white other than the color filling his full cheeks. "It's Mádl Ferenc."

"What about him?"

Mádl Ferenc is the new president of the Republic of Hungary. Out of nowhere, he won the presidency. Nobody expected it. In fact, there were some questions about its legitimacy. During his campaign, he promised to shake things up. He believed Hungary wasn't taking full advantage of the opportunities now afforded to us following the dismantling of the Berlin Wall and the Russian withdrawal.

Laci looks back down at the desk. "He's openly campaigning against you now. He's rallying support to supplant you. He wants you out."

I turn and walk back to the window. None of this is a surprise. I've been expecting it. I've wondered why it's taken so long. Weeks ago, the president came to Laci and told him of his plans. He hoped I would give up and throw in the towel after Laci told me. But President Mádl doesn't know who he's dealing with. If he wants me out, he'll see I won't go quietly, and I still have a few tricks up my sleeve.

"Who's he been talking to?"

"Who hasn't he been talking to? Members of parliament, local leaders, even the press."

That brings my gaze away from the window. "What?"

Laci nods. "I don't know that for sure. But it seems likely his office is leaking information to the press."

"What kind of information?"

"Statistical information."

I feel a flash of irritation. "I'm proud of my record as director. The streets of Budapest, and Hungary as a whole, have never been safer. Violent crime is down, along with suicide and theft. You name it. It's better to be a Hungarian now than ever before."

Laci stands from the chair and raises his palms to me. "Oh, I agree. I'm your biggest fan, you know that. You don't have to convince me."

I shrug. "Then why would he leak statistical information? If he wants me out, that's going to do the opposite."

Laci looks down. "There's one measurement that hasn't fallen. It's actually increased and continues to." He looks up at me as I feel myself glaring back at him, daring him to finish.

"What measurement?"

He looks away, and his voice lowers. "Missing persons. Specifically teen girls."

I give a curt nod.

He tells me again that he's here for me. That he will help in any way he can. I thank him and walk him out of my office. After I shut the door, I walk back to my desk. But before I sit down, I slam my palm on the surface. It stings, but I embrace it. Things are going to hurt more before they get better.

Chapter Twelve

Lili

I walk into the office and head to my cubicle. I'm late, but I'm hoping nobody has noticed. Yesterday, Tibor and I visited Herend for a special "Shopping Queen" segment that will air this weekend. Herend is a little town near Lake Balaton in Western Hungary. I didn't want to go. Although the town is known worldwide for the porcelain they manufacture, there isn't much else there. It makes for a whole lot of time in the van looking at nothing.

I'm not one of those girls who has always dreamed of owning my own porcelain dishes. And I definitely have no interest in porcelain dolls. But I must admit, the factory and tour were beautiful and fascinating. We walked through a step-by-step explanation of the manufacturing process. I couldn't believe the skill of the women who molded the porcelain and painted it. We got some beautiful shots, and I know our news director will love it. I'm glad I went.

It's a good thing. He's been on me about "not staying in my lane." So what if I don't love shopping like he thinks I should. I do my job. I go and act perky and happy. I play my part as the cute blond girl who loves to shop. Nobody can tell I'm bored out of my mind. I'll keep being the "Shopping Queen." But if he would just give me a chance, I know I could prove myself to him. I'm much more than just a pretty face. I'd be even better at reporting on real issues. Things I actually care about. He'd move me over to the investigatory team in a second.

As I pass Anna, she looks up from her computer and gives me a disapproving look.

"What?" I ask.

She looks down at her watch and back up at me.

"I know, I know. We got back late from Herend, and I hit snooze too many times."

I enter my cubicle, set down my bag, and power on my computer. While it boots up, I lean my head over the side of the booth so I can see her.

"Has anyone been asking for me?"

She looks at me and nods.

"Who? Attila?"

She bites the side of her cheek and nods again.

"What did you say?"

"I told him he should fire you. That you suck at your job anyway."

I stare at her in shock when she starts laughing.

"Just kidding. He never came looking for you."

"You brat," I say, smacking her and rolling back to my side of the cubicle.

I pick up the telephone and hear the familiar beeps indicating I have messages. I dial my passcode and wait for the robotic voice to finish telling me I have two messages. The first is my mother. "Lili, this is the third time I've called. Is this even working? I need to talk to you. Call me." I roll my eyes and hit the delete button. I know I need to call her; I just don't want to. Every time I talk to her, it's the same. Her knee hurts. Her hips hurt. She saw me on TV talking about some shopping segment and thought my hair was in my face too much. It's exhausting.

When the second message plays, the voice is unfamiliar, making me sit forward in my chair. "Lili, my name is Béla. I'm a reporter with the *Magyar Hírlap*. You left me a message about a story I wrote regarding a missing teenage girl from Pápa. Sounds like we might be able to work together. Give me a call, and we can talk." He repeats his number, and I write it down on a notepad next to the phone. I hang up, stand from my chair, and look over the cubicles around me. One of the advantages of being tall is I can easily see who's at their desks. Only Anna would be able to hear me. She'll disapprove, but she won't talk. I sit back down and dial the number. After a couple rings, Béla picks up.

"Hi, Béla. This is Lili from Duna Television."

"Oh, yes, Lili. You got my message. Sorry it took me a few days to reply."

"No problem."

A silence falls, and I realize I better get to the point. I drop my voice to barely above a whisper.

"Um...I called because I saw your article on the missing girl from Pápa. Do you know if she's been found?"

"No, she hasn't. At least not as of last night."

"Any idea where she went? What happened to her?"

"Nope. But something is going on."

"What do you mean?"

"She's not the only one. I'm about to go to press with another story today. A girl was visiting from London and hasn't been seen in a week."

I can feel my heart rate quicken. "Same age?"

"A year older. She came with some friends. They were staying in an apartment. After not seeing her for a few hours, they went to the room she was in, and she was gone. No trace of her. Aren't you guys reporting on any of this?"

We probably are. But I'm not.

"Yeah, we are. I've also received the same reports. But I'm looking for someone I can interview. A source I can use."

He's silent for a few seconds. "I don't know that I can help you there. The cops won't say anything. And I did talk to a girl who was taken and found. But she wouldn't say much and didn't want to go on the record with anything."

"Maybe I can try. Maybe she'd feel more comfortable talking to me."

"Maybe...what's your email? I'll send you her contact information. You can give it a shot. Just don't tell her you got it from me."

After repeating the email, we agree to talk again and hang up. I turn to my computer, enter my password, and open the browser. I can feel eyes on me.

"What are you doing?"

I turn and look at her. "You know what I'm doing."

Her chin rests on the top of the cubicle, and she rolls her eyes but surprisingly says nothing and just drops back down on her side of the wall.

I pull up my email, and I'm surprised to see I already have a message from Béla. As promised, he's given me the girl's phone number and address. I pick up the receiver and punch the numbers into my phone. After a short pause, I hear the phone ring.

"Hello?"

"Hi, hello. Is this Renata?"

"No, hold on. Let me get her."

I hear the phone being set down and the girl calling for Renata. After a minute, she comes on the line. "Hello?"

"Hi, Renata. You don't know me. My name is Lili. I'm a reporter with Duna Television."

A hesitation on the other end of the line. "Yes?"

"I wondered if you'd be willing to meet me. I'll buy you a cup of coffee."

"Why? What's this about?"

I was really hoping she wouldn't ask that. "Well...I heard what happened to you, and I wondered if you wouldn't mind telling me about it."

"No, I don't want to talk about it."

I hear a fumble on the other end of the line. It sounds like she's about to hang up.

"Don't go, please?"

Silence on the other end, and I'm worried she's already gone.

"Look, I just want you to tell me your story, not on TV or anything. I won't share it without your permission. You could help other girls like you. I'm trying to help them."

I can hear her breathing into the phone.

"When?"

The relief is so substantial I can almost taste it. "How's tomorrow for you?"

"I've got school and work."

"Another day then?"

"Thursday. But I'll only meet at the café near my apartment. Do you know the Madal Café?

I don't, but I'm not going to kill the momentum. "Yes."

"I can meet at eight a.m."

"Great!"

"And I'm going to bring my friend. She has to be there too."

"No problem. Whatever will work for you."

We say goodbye and hang up, and I lean back in my chair. I'm beaming.

"Who are you meeting?"

Anna's looking at me again, her chin on the cubicle wall.

I wink at her. "Someone who's going to give me a great shopping story."

I don't know how she does it because her chin never leaves the top of the cubicle, but she shakes her head. Or maybe she doesn't, and I just imagine it. Her head disappears again, and I sit staring at my screen, thinking. This is my chance to report on something that actually matters, and I'm not going to waste it.

Chapter Thirteen

Peter

Peter looks up at the buildings so tall they block out the sun and can't help feeling like he's home. Budapest is a big city, with two million people, but it's only a fifth of the size of New York. Today is his first full day back since he left a little over a year ago. He was a fish out of water when he first returned to Hungary. Although he grew up in the country, he hadn't been back in over thirty years. He lived in the United States longer than in Hungary. But, after a few weeks, he became more comfortable. He felt a little strange speaking Hungarian all the time. He found it odd that, at times, his mouth would hurt. Maybe hurt isn't the proper term. His mouth felt fatigued. People don't realize they use different muscles when they speak other languages, especially those as diverse as Hungarian and English. In those thirty years in New York City, he spoke Hungarian maybe ten times. Being a native Hungarian, he could still speak. But his vocabulary was limited. There were words he had forgotten or never learned.

Now, being back in NYC, walking along Fifty-First Street, he feels a mix of excitement and dread. He's headed to his old station, the Seventeenth Precinct. As he grows closer, memories flood his mind. Most are good. His first staff meeting, for example. As a new officer he was forced to sing "Hey Jude" on a table in front of the whole precinct. His first arrest. A gangbanger who shot up a neighborhood. Peter was able to identify him and bring him in without incident. The best memory took place a few years later. He was asked to meet with the chief of detectives, unusual for a uniformed police officer. He was expecting a reprimand. While helping at a crime scene, he noticed a discrepancy in the account of one of the eyewitnesses. He pointed it out to the lead detective, and the detective sent him home. Berating him and telling him to leave the real police work to the real police. The next day he received the meeting request. As he walked into the chief's office, he worried he might be fired. His jaw nearly hit the ground when the chief informed him he'd be promoted. He was asked to be a part of the Special Investigations Division of the NYPD. He'd be elevated to detective.

He reaches the front door of the precinct and nods to the two officers standing outside, smoking. One of them looks somewhat familiar. *I wonder how much things have changed.* He pulls the door open and steps inside. A face he's seen thousands of times looks at him while talking on the phone. She frowns, then says into the phone, "Can you hold, please?" She pushes a button on the switchboard and stands from her desk. She walks around it with her arms outstretched. "Oh, my gosh, I never thought I would see you again."

She rushes into Peter's arms.

"How are you, Sally?"

"I'm good. We sure miss you around here. Are you coming back to work? I heard you went back to Czechoslovakia?"

He's not surprised to hear her get the country wrong. To anyone outside of Europeans, Eastern Europe might as well be another planet. They had about the same chance of picking out Pluto as pointing out Hungary on a map.

"Hungary, actually. I still live there. I just came back to visit. I missed you guys."

From behind, Peter hears a voice boom out, "Doth my eyes deceive me? Is that who I think it is?"

Peter would recognize that voice anywhere. It's Tony Caruso, his partner of four years. Tony is a wiz at mimicking voices. This time he says it as if he's Patrick Stewart in *Star Trek*. Tony grew up across the river and has a distinct Brooklyn accent, when he's not impersonating famous actors. Peter turns to look at him as he heads his way. Tony's dressed in a blue button-down shirt; the sleeves rolled up to his elbows. He's always been thick, probably all that Italian food he eats. He's not obese, but he could stand to lose a few pounds. The kind of guy who's thick all over. He's shorter than Peter, about five foot nine. His hair was just starting to sprout gray strands when they were partners. *Looks like it's progressed in the last year.*

Tony reaches him, and Peter extends his hand. He ignores it, grabs Peter in a bear hug, and thumps him on the back. Before he knows it, Peter's surrounded by cops. Many familiar faces, a few not so familiar. He receives a plethora of hugs, handshakes, and pats on the back.

Finally, after a few minutes of people asking about what he's been up to and several telling him about the goings-on over the last year, people begin to back away. Peter surveys the faces one more time and frowns. His oldest friend, Lieutenant Bridges, is nowhere to be found. Tony takes it as an opportunity to pull him aside. He leads him to one of the interrogation rooms just off the block of cubicles. Peter takes the interviewee's seat while Tony sits across the table. This is a room Peter's been in a couple hundred times. But never in this seat.

Tony breaks the silence. "Couldn't stay away, huh? Had to come home?"

"I'm only on a visit. I'm going back."

Tony waves his meaty hand. "That's fine for them out there. But be honest with me. You missed it, didn't you? The city. The job."

Peter shakes his head and looks down. "I don't miss the job. I do miss the city. Especially L'Angeletto's. It's funny, Hungary is way closer to Italy than New York, but the Italian food there doesn't compare to here."

Tony puffs out his chest, a smile from ear to ear. "The city has better food than Italy. All the best Italians came here. You've had my mom's cooking."

Peter chuckles. "You're probably right."

"Wait a second. Did you just say I'm right? Let me get out my recorder. I think that's the first time you've admitted it."

Peter shakes his head, and they laugh.

After a beat, Peter looks at him. "How have you been? How are Carla and the kids?"

Tony puts his hand to his forehead and blows out his breath. "Why did I ever think getting married and having kids was a good idea?" After saying it, his face goes white, realizing what he's said. He holds up a hand. "I'm sorry, Peter. I didn't mean—"

Peter waves him off. "It's okay. Don't worry about it."

They fall silent again, and Tony looks away.

"So, how are things? How's your new partner?"

Tony shifts in his chair. "Eh...okay. She thinks she knows everything. Graduated from the academy a few years back with high honors and all that. I keep telling her you don't learn to be a detective in a textbook or through simulations. You taught me that."

Peter shrugs. That's partially true. He might have said something like that. But science has always played a role in good police work. And that intel is becoming more and more critical. "What are you working on now?"

Tony leans back. "A racketeering gig. A real estate agent who's been misusing his client's escrow funds. Or I should say 'allegedly.' But it's an open-and-shut case. He's guilty."

Peter turns and stares at the wall before he looks back at Tony, watching him carefully. "Hey, whatever happened to Kaminski?"

"Who?"

"You know, Kaminski. The cop was put on leave and investigated because his gun showed up in a murder case. I was working on that case before Karen died. Remember? I was thinking about it the other day and wondered how it shook out."

Peter's acting nonchalant, as if he just thought of it. But this is precisely why he came into the precinct. Peter and Tony had been partners for over four years and had seen each other nearly every day. He can read him like a book, and he's watching him closely. The movement is subtle; most detectives wouldn't even see it. But Peter isn't like most detectives. Tony stiffens, his breathing shifts, and his eyes narrow before he looks up at the ceiling. "Oh, yeah…That's a sad situation, actually."

"How so?"

"The guy's dead."

Peter can feel his pulse quicken. "Dead? How? He was young."

Tony shakes his head. "Suicide, man. He hung himself. I think his wife found him."

Peter leans back and looks up at the ceiling, exhaling. "That's terrible." He means it. But not for the reason Tony thinks. "Do you have his address?"

Tony frowns and gives Peter a curious look.

"Oh, I just want to send condolences to his wife. I knew him a bit. I'd like to let her know how sorry I am."

Tony nods but continues to look at Peter curiously.

"I know something about what she's going through. Even when I didn't know the people, it was nice to hear others were mindful of me."

Tony smiles and stands, patting Peter on the shoulder. "I miss you, man. You're a really good guy. Let's go find that address."

Chapter Fourteen

Zsuzsa

I step off the streetcar and catch a glimpse of myself in the shop window. I'm wearing a long black coat with black heels and black gloves. Although elegant, I wonder if I look like I'm headed to a funeral rather than a date. This is my favorite coat, mostly because I think it makes me look thinner than I am. Last night Gábor called me to confirm the details of our date. He offered to pick me up, but I told him I would prefer to meet at the restaurant.

After a three-minute walk, I reach the restaurant. I'm surprised to find Gábor standing out front. As I look at him, I'm reminded again of just how gorgeous he is. His dark, wavy hair is perfectly arranged. He's wearing a dark suit with a red tie. He sees me and smiles, and I can't help blushing. I look down as I approach.

"*Szia,*" he says, flashing me a broad smile.

"Helló."

He opens the door for me, and I thank him. After we're inside, he approaches the hostess. She's a slender woman. Tall with dark, almost black hair and full lips. Her eyes sparkle as she looks at him. It's not just because he's a customer. She glances at me but only in passing. Her eyes are drawn to Gábor. He tells her his name, and she looks at the list on the stand. She smiles and invites us to follow her. Gábor lets me go before him. We walk through the restaurant and are shown our table along the window. She turns, looks past me, and asks him if the table will do. He looks at me, and I tell her it will be fine. She offers to take my coat and gloves.

I'm wearing a strapless red dress, and after taking off my coat and handing it to her, I catch Gábor admiring it. He helps me into my seat and takes the chair across from me. She hands us menus and wishes us a pleasant evening.

"You look fabulous," he tells me.

"You look pretty good yourself. I'm impressed you matched your tie to my dress."

He chuckles. "What can I say? I'm good. Have you been here before?"

I shake my head.

"They're known most for their Tokaji wine. And the atmosphere." He waves his hand, and I look out at our fellow diners. The architecture is beautiful, with ornate wooden arches throughout the dining hall. Voluminous chandeliers dangle from the ceiling. If he's trying to impress me, it's working. I'm not sure I've ever felt this fancy.

Over the next thirty minutes, we chat about growing up. He tells me about his sister, his marriage, and his son. I tell him about bartending, my parents, and my dreams of being a detective. He has a way of looking at me, making me feel like I'm all that matters. Nothing I say is that interesting, but to look at his face, you would think I'm teaching him how to save the world. Our server returns with our main course. I ordered the filet of pork tenderloin while he got the sirloin steak with the spicy duck-liver mousse.

"Can I ask you something?" I look up at him and nod. "Why did you hesitate to go out with me?"

"What? You're so used to women falling all over themselves to go out with you that my hesitation caught you off guard?"

He doesn't know my sassy personality, and the question flusters him. "Uh...no. I mean."

I laugh my usual boisterous laugh, and several people turn to look at us. I duck my head and smile. "I'm teasing you."

I can see the relief in his eyes, and he takes a drink of wine.

"Seriously, though. Why?"

I'm unsure how much I want to tell him, but I can't come up with something better to say. "Well, I've been dating someone else."

He nods and continues watching me with those piercing eyes.

"Is it serious?"

"It can't be that serious, can it? I'm here with you tonight."

He smiles, and I notice a cleft in his chin.

"I'm glad you are. You look amazing in that dress."

I feel myself blush, and I take another bite of tenderloin.

"So, are you still dating him?"

"Let's just say it's complicated." I can tell he wants to ask more but has the good sense not to. "Anyway, do you want me to think about him or you?"

He raises his hands and smiles. "I was just thinking, didn't you have some advertising questions you wanted to ask me?"

We continue to eat and talk. True to his word, he lets me ask him advertising advice. He really is a wealth of knowledge, and judging by the restaurant, I assume he does well for himself.

After we finish, he walks me out. His hand is on the small of my back. He's a perfect gentleman helping me with my coat and getting the door. When we reach the exit, I turn and extend my hand. "Thanks for a lovely evening."

He takes it and asks, "Can I drive you home?"

I look up at that gorgeous face. I shouldn't, but I want to. Finally, I nod. He smiles and tells me he'll get the car and meet me out front. Quick as a cat, he's through the door and out of sight. A couple minutes later, he pulls up to the curb in a red BMW M Coupe. I wonder if he always matches his tie to his car. Before I can reach the vehicle, he's come around and opened the door for me. After I'm settled in the seat, I give him my address, and he drives.

I'm surprised when I see he's headed south on Bécsi Utca, but I don't say anything, curious to see where he's taking us. After two blocks, he turns right on Rákóczi Utca, and I can see we're headed in the right direction now. He has the radio low, but I'd recognize this song anywhere. It's one of my favorites, and I have to fight the urge to reach over and turn it up. It's Hungarian. We Hungarians listen to a lot of American music, but some Hungarian bands have done well here at home. This band, Republic, is one of them. The name of the song is "Csillagok, Csillagok" ("Stars, Stars"). It's a love song. Before I know it, I find myself humming along. He looks at me, smiles, then turns it up.

"You like Republic?" he asks.

"I love them. This is one of my favorite songs."

He smiles at me with this funny look in his eye. He turns back to the road, tilts his head back, and starts belting out the lyrics with surprising force. "*Merre jár, hol lehet most a kedvesem, Veszélyes út, amin jársz, veszélyes út, amin járok, Egyszer te is hazatalálsz, egyszer én is hazatalálok.*" ("Where are you going, where is my love now? Dangerous road you're on, dangerous road I'm on. One day you will find home, one day I will find home too.")

He's taken me completely off guard by the outburst, and I look away. I concentrate on a building we're passing fighting the urge to laugh. He's so confident yet he's so bad. Not a single note is on key. He's probably lived his whole life believing he can sing, and nobody has ever been honest with him.

He goes on singing the rest of the song. When he finishes, he turns the radio back down. I can sense him looking at me. I turn back to him and smile, trying not to laugh. I can tell he wants me to say something. Praise him. But I can't do it. I just can't lie to him.

"It's a great song," I say.

He agrees. After a few seconds, he can see I'm not going to say anything else. His face falls before asking me what other music I like, and we fall into a discussion about bands and popular music. Fifteen minutes later, we pull up to my apartment building. I thank him for a lovely evening and reach for the handle. He asks me to wait, gets out, and walks around the car. He opens the door for me and helps me out. The car sits low, and it's a little awkward with my heels. He has my hand and doesn't let go as he walks me up. After reaching the top of the stairs, we turn to face each other. He wastes no time getting to the point.

"Will you go out with me again?"

I lower my lashes under his scrutinizing gaze. "Probably."

He frowns and tips his head to the side.

"Probably? How can I convince you?"

He's leaning close, and I feel so nervous. I like him. But this is too fast. He takes another step closer, and I take a step back. "I'm sorry. This is a little quick for me."

"No, I'm sorry," he says. "I like you and—"

"It's okay. Call me in a few days if you want to go out again. Let me think about it."

He agrees, and we exchange a hug before I enter the building. After hitting the elevator call button, I turn and notice him. He's still standing on the steps, watching me. I wave and enter the elevator, leaving him standing outside.

Chapter Fifteen

Detective Szabo

The phone next to me buzzes, and I pick it up. I'm not in a good mood, and my tone illustrates it. "Yes, this is Detective Szabo of the Hungarian National Police."

"Detective Szabo," says a female voice.

I sigh. Isn't that what I just said? "Yes, this is Detective Szabo. How can I help you?"

"Are you the detective in charge of the human-trafficking task force?"

I'm wary now. "Yes."

"My name is Horvath Lili. I'm a reporter with Duna Television."

"No comment."

"Sir, I didn't ask anything."

"Well, whatever you plan to ask, I have no comment." Usually, this takes the wind out of the reporter's sails. But this girl is different.

"Sir, I have information that you imprisoned another officer in your task force. That he's been blamed for murdering the former head of the task force, Kovacs Lajos."

This stops me dead. How does she know this? Who has she been talking to? I sit contemplating these questions.

"Sir? Are you there?"

I clear my throat but still hesitate before answering. "We're holding no officer under suspicion of murder. The death of Kovacs Lajos is still an active investigation."

"So you are no longer holding anyone for his murder?"

"That's correct." I wince after I say it.

"But you were holding someone? And you do believe it was murder?"

"Ma'am, as I told you before, I have no comment. Please don't call again."

I slam down the phone, lean back in my chair, and stare at the wall. How did she know that? Someone must have told her we arrested Peter, but who? It couldn't be Peter. If she talked to him, she would know they let him go. Zsuzsa?

My eyes narrow as I look at the clock on the wall. Five minutes after nine a.m. I'm late to my own meeting. I stand from my desk and walk out into the bullpen area. It's empty. Everyone's in the conference room waiting for me. I cross the room, reach for the door, and thrust it open. Seated around the table are detectives Varga and Farkas. Director Toth is also here, along with a man I don't recognize. Toth and I make eye contact, and I can tell by the look on his face he isn't pleased. I walk to the front of the table next to the whiteboard. Varga and Farkas sit on either side of the table across from each other. Toth is at the other end with the stranger seated to his right.

"Sorry, I'm late," I say as I put a few files on the table in front of me. "Director, I see we have a guest?"

Now it's not just his demeanor but his tone that tells me I'm not high on his list today. "Yes, Detective. Had you been on time, you would know this is newly promoted Detective Katona. Detective Katona is now a member of the task force, replacing Detective Kovacs." He turns to Katona. "Detective, why don't you stand and introduce yourself."

This revelation surprises and annoys me. He made me the head of the task force after Kovacs was killed. Shouldn't I have a say in who joins us?

Katona stands, and I realize I've seen him before. He was there on the bridge after the accident that killed Kovacs. He was one of the uniformed police officers on the scene. I didn't recognize him because now he's not wearing a police officer uniform. He's dressed in a crisp white shirt, a bright-blue tie, and black pants. He looks like Burt Reynolds, mustache and all. He's even got a cocky demeanor like him. They could be twins.

"Thank you, Director," he begins. "It's a pleasure to serve with each of you." He looks at each of us in turn. "As the director said, I'm new to detective work. But certainly not new to police work. I began my career as a city police officer. For the last three years, I've worked for the National Police, primarily with the violent-crime unit. I'm a native of Budapest, having grown up in Újpest."

He sits down, and the director smiles at him, then looks back at me. The smile vanishes. I take that as my cue to get the meeting started.

"Again, I'm sorry I was late. Detective Katona, welcome. I'm sure I can speak for Varga and Farkas and tell you we're glad to have the additional help." Both Varga and Farkas nod. I turn to the whiteboard and write three names in large letters before turning back to the group. "These three names represent three new girls reported missing in the last week. All of whom are either foreign or from the country. We can't confirm it, but I think it's safe to assume they've been taken by the human-trafficking circuit operating in the city."

I walk to the files I have stacked on the table, open the top one, and take out several sheets of paper. Each are photocopies of the files made for the missing women. I pass them to Varga and ask her to distribute them around the table. I wait, giving them time to review the information. "We've been tracking the abductors for months now, with little success. I think it's time for us to do something different."

Each person looks up from the paper they're holding. I've got their attention now.

"In the past, we planted a male officer with Andras. He was able to get close but ultimately blew his cover to save a couple people." I point to Varga. "We planted Varga in the club and were able to get the traffickers to take the bait. But we made a mistake. We arrested them too early. I understand why Kovacs did it. He was protecting Varga. But it was the wrong decision. We should have allowed her to be taken. And we could have tracked her with this."

I hold up a small disk-shaped item, similar in size to a hundred-forint coin. "This uses GPS technology to track anywhere it goes. I can't tell you how it works, but I've seen it demonstrated, and I know that it does. It's time we get bolder in our efforts. We need to find a suitable candidate, someone who can handle being taken. She needs to serve as adequate bait. Someone like Varga."

Farkas raises his hand, and I call on him. "But we don't know where they're operating now."

I hold up my finger and wink at him. "That used to be true, until now. Look closer at each of those sheets in your hands."

They study the papers and, one by one, they raise their eyes back to me, understanding coming to them.

"Each was last seen at a club in the Belváros. It's a perfect spot, right in the center of the city. It's a favorite of tourists. We know the traffickers like to target foreign women. Women who aren't from Budapest and won't be immediately missed. Now we just need to find the right candidate."

Katona raises his hand. "Is there a particular look? What makes the perfect candidate?"

"Young and pretty," Farkas says. "Like Varga."

"So why don't we just use Varga again?" Katona asks.

The director speaks for the first time. "Because we already used her. They'll know her. Or at least they might. We can't run that risk."

"Exactly," I say.

Katona nods. "I think I might know someone. She looks a lot like Varga. She's a cop with the city. I worked with her for a few months. She's young and very pretty."

"Great!" I say. "Let's bring her in. I'd like to talk to her."

Chapter Sixteen

Peter

Peter sits in Gary's spare bedroom, staring at the phone. The time in Hungary is six hours ahead of New York. It's four p.m. in New York making it ten p.m. in Hungary. If he's going to call her today, he's got to call now. But should he? Toth knows about Szép Ilona's. He likely has the phones tapped. He can't risk calling her there. But what about her home? Could his call put her at risk? It wouldn't be the first time a call from him put her life in danger. But he has to get a message to her. He has to let Zsuzsa know he's out of jail.

He picks up the phone and dials the long phone number starting with the country code. He raises the receiver to his ear and listens to it ring. After multiple buzzes, the answering machine picks up. He hangs up. He can't risk leaving a message. He sets down the phone and walks out of the room and down the hall. His sister-in-law, Becky, is fixing dinner. His niece, Rachel, is doing homework at the kitchen table.

"Hey," Becky says, "here he is. You can ask him now."

"Ask me what?" Peter says.

Rachel turned twelve a few weeks ago and is in middle school. She and his daughter were the same age. They were only weeks apart. Every time he looks at Rachel, he's reminded of his daughter and the loss. It's painful.

"Uncle Peter?"

"Yes." She seems hesitant. Odd. She's a confident girl. Sometimes too confident. "What is it?"

"Could you help me with my homework?"

"Sure."

"Except...I don't know if you can. I don't know if you know anything about it."

Peter frowns and looks at Becky. She rolls her eyes and turns back to the stove. Peter looks at Rachel again, and she's frowning now.

"Do you think you could?"

Peter sits at the table. "I don't know. What's the subject?"

Rachel looks down, not meeting his gaze. Her voice has gone soft. "It's about feelings."

Peter's anxiety rises. Is she going to want to talk about loss? Depression? Get him to open up about the death of his wife. The loss of his daughter? He loves his niece, but this isn't a discussion he wants to have with her right now.

"What feelings?" he asks warily.

Rachel shrugs. "Hungry feelings."

Peter looks at Becky, but she has her back to him. She shakes her head again. Rachel can't hold it now, and a laugh escapes her lips. She erupts into a peal of giggles.

Peter playfully smacks the table. "You know, Rachel. Rather than learning about feelings, I think you need to learn to spell."

This stops her giggles, and she looks at him curiously. "What?"

"Hungary is spelled with an *a* in the word. Your teacher wants you to learn about the country, not the feeling. If you were better at spelling, you'd know that."

"Hey," she says, knowing she's being teased. "I got second place in the spelling bee last year."

He smiles at her. "What word got you out? *Male*?"

Becky laughs, and Rachel frowns, clearly not getting the joke.

Peter waves a hand. "So you want to learn about Hungary, huh?"

She nods. "We had to pick a country to do a report on, and I thought I'd do Hungary."

"Sounds good. What do you want to know?"

"Who are the Mag-yars?"

She says it so badly Peter winces. "First off, it's not Mag-yars. It's Mag-yars. The *gy* in any Hungarian word is pronounced like the letter *j* in English. That's what Hungarians call themselves. In America, we call them Hungarians, but they call themselves the Magyars."

"Hmm," she says and writes in her notepad. "So, who are they?"

"What do you mean? You're looking at one."

She presses her lips together like she had never considered that. "You're a Magyar?"

"What? You thought I was an alien?"

She smiles. "No, I just think of you as an American."

He chuckles. "Well, I've lived in America longer than Hungary. But my name is Andrássy Péter. Here, let me show you." He takes the pencil from her and writes his name as he was taught in Hungarian school. He can't help but laugh at the awe in her eyes.

"But why did you write Andrassy first?"

"Because surname, or family name, comes first in Hungarian. The given name comes second. Have you heard of Zsa Zsa Gabor and the Gabor sisters?" She nods. "In Hungary, you would say her name as Gábor Sári. I bet your teacher doesn't even know that."

She smiles and has him write the name on her notepad.

"So, who are you?"

He chuckles. "What do you mean?"

Her cheeks fill with color. "I mean, who are the Magyars?" This time she says it right.

"That's an excellent question. They just kind of showed up in Europe around theninth century. They lived in an area that would probably be modern-day Mongolia. For some reason, they left and conquered armies until they stopped in the Carpathian Basin in the middle of Europe. That's why Hungarian is unlike any other language spoken around them. Seven countries border Hungary, but none speak a language remotely similar. Magyars aren't native Europeans."

Rachel fires questions at him for the next twenty minutes while Becky fixes dinner. Gary comes home, and they eat.

As they near the end of the meal, Peter looks at Rachel. "You remember how I helped you with your homework?" She looks at him like he's losing his mind. "How about helping me with mine?"

She frowns. "Uncle Peter, you don't have homework."

"Okay, well, it's not homework. But see that machine over there?" He points to the computer at the desk in the office. "I bet you're a lot better at using it than I am. Maybe you can help me find something."

She nods enthusiastically and rises from the table.

"Wait, only as long as it's okay with your parents."

"Of course," Gary says.

Peter and Rachel take their dishes to the sink, wash them, and put them in the dishwasher, then head into the office. Rachel makes Peter sit in the driving chair. She pulls another chair around, relishing the opportunity to teach her uncle something.

"Would you be able to pull up news from Hungary?" he asks.

"Hmm, I think so."

She leans over him and takes the mouse. She double-clicks the big blue *E*, just like the girl from the internet café from weeks ago in Budapest. After a few minutes of searching, he stops her. On the homepage of the *Magyar Hírlap*, he sees something that startles him. It's an article written by Nagy Béla.

"Can you save this page?" he asks.

"Sure."

He thanks her and tells her he can take it from here. The title of the article is "Missing Girls." In the article, Béla points out several girls who have gone missing in Budapest. Some are foreign. Peter's mind races as he reads the report. The implications are significant. If the media begins to latch on to this, what does that mean for the traffickers? For Toth? It also might mean this Béla could be in danger.

Two hours later, Peter stands from the computer and walks back down the hallway to the guest room. It's midnight in Budapest now, but he doesn't care. He dials the number, and the phone rings. This time a voice comes on the line.

"Helló?"

"Kata? This is Peter."

"Peter?"

"Andrássy Péter."

"Oh, Peter. Are you okay? How are you calling me?"

"I don't want to be on the phone long. But I had to get a message to you and Zsuzsa. I'm no longer in Hungary. I'm in New York City."

"How did you get out of jail?"

"It's a long story. Do you have an email address? It's not safe for us to be on the phone long. Do you have a paper? Right down this address and email me. Do it from a public place, like an internet café. I'll explain everything. And please, tell Zsuzsa."

Chapter Seventeen

Director Toth

"Dad, does that man over there know you?"

I look across the restaurant to where my daughter is pointing and see Sandor János, the speaker of the National Assembly of Hungary. He's dining with his wife, and when he sees me, he smiles and nods.

"Yes, that's a friend." I look at my wife. "I'm going to go over and say hello."

"József, do you have to? The server will be back with our food. Can't you be out with your family one night?"

I stand from my seat as my wife and daughter glare at me. "I won't be longer than five minutes." I walk across the room, and János stands as I approach, his hand extended.

He's a nice-looking man, with dark-brown hair and light-green eyes. He's in his late forties, and although I'm taller than he is, his slender build makes him seem taller than he actually is.

"Director, it's so nice to see you."

"You also, Mr. Speaker." I look at his wife, and she extends her hand to me. I take it, letting my lips brush the back. She's a lovely woman with short blond hair, blue eyes, and perfectly defined features. They make a striking duo. No wonder they're considered one of the most, if not the most, powerful political couples in Hungary. I release her hand and smile before turning back to János. "Do you have a moment?"

He looks at his wife, and she nods. We walk away from the table in search of a more secluded space. When we reach the back of the dining hall, I lean close to him and speak in a low voice. "You know why I want to talk to you?"

His look tells me everything I need to know. He keeps his eyes trained on me.

"Has he contacted you?"

"Of course."

"What did he say?"

He shrugs. "Probably exactly what you've heard. He wants you out as director." János hesitates now and shifts his weight. "He's grateful for your service. But he thinks you've been in the position too long. He wants one of his people. Someone he chooses."

"Who?"

"He didn't say."

I nod and look back toward the other restaurant patrons. "And what do you think?"

He puts his hand on my shoulder. "József, I think you've been wonderful for the city and the country. Under your leadership, crime has fallen in most of the major categories. For many of us, the country is safer. I told the president that."

"And what did he say?"

"He agreed. And then he showed me an article written yesterday in the *Magyar Hírlap*. Have you seen it?"

I chew the inside of my lip and nod.

"You know as well as anyone that the president is blamed for things he has no control over. And sometimes, he's given credit for other things he has little to do with. But ultimately, if there's a problem in the country, he's held responsible." He squeezes my shoulder as I stare out at the restaurant crowd. "If you want my advice, deal with the abductions. Particularly the foreign ones. If the media stops reporting on it, President Mádl will back off, and you may be able to keep your job." I look at him and nod, my mind working. "I should get back to my wife. She'll be wondering about me." He turns to go, then turns back to me. "József, you have many supporters. He won't push for a new director if the pressure comes off him." He looks me in the eye, and we nod at each other. He heads back to his wife, and I visit the restroom.

I return to the table, and my wife gives me a look. The food has already been delivered, and it's getting cold. We eat while my wife and daughter do most of the talking. I only speak when spoken to; even then, they have to prompt me for an answer. After the meal, we have a quiet drive home. When we enter the house, our daughter heads to her room, hopefully, to do homework. I walk into the kitchen to get a drink of water. The steak I had was prepared well but oversalted. My wife follows me into the kitchen.

"Was that the speaker of the National Assembly?"

I nod as I take several big gulps.

"What did you talk to him about?"

Our eyes lock, and I know I can't sidestep the question this time. She won't accept a brushoff.

"President Mádl is campaigning against me. He wants a new leader for the National Police."

She gasps and steps closer. "But...why?"

I shake my head. "It's all politics. He and I are from different political parties. He wants his own guy in there." She raises her hand to her face, and I can see it trembling. She doesn't handle bad news well. Maybe I shouldn't have told her, but then again, this might buy me some distance. She'll understand why I'm less attentive to her and Ildiko. I put my cup in the sink and turn back to her. I take her in my arms. "It's okay. I have a lot of support from other powerful people. I just need to rally them to my side." I step back and look her in the eyes. "I've got to make a few calls. Don't wait up for me."

I walk down the hall to my home office and shut the door behind me. I sit at the desk and wait until I hear her move down the hallway toward our bedroom. Once the door closes, I pick up the phone and dial a number. After a couple rings, the voice answers.

"It's me. What's the latest with our boy in America?"

"He's back in New York City. He's staying with his family there."

"Is he going to stay put? He can't come back here."

"He won't. And if he does, we'll know about it."

I lean back in my chair and put my feet up on the desk. "What about the bartender? Has he tried to contact her?"

"Not yet. It looks like he meant what he said in the jail."

I lean forward and pick a pen off the desktop. I start tapping it on my leg. I don't buy it. He went to Ukraine for her. "There's something else I need you to do."

"What?"

"I need you to contact the reporter with the *Magyar Hírlap*. See if he can be persuaded to stop writing about abductions."

"What kind of persuasion? Are we talking threats or bribes or something else?"

I sigh. "Let's start with bribes. See what his price is."

"You got it, Boss. How high do you want me to go?"

"Up to a hundred thousand. But make sure he'll really stop. Dangle a threat."

Chapter Eighteen

Lili

It's 8:05 a.m. Thursday morning, and I'm late. I can see the sign for the Madal Café on the other side of the street. I don't do mornings. Well, intentionally, that is. Sometimes I have no choice. At least I'm walking into a coffee shop. With any luck, I'll soon have a large cup of caffeine in my hands. I push the heavy glass door open and step inside.

It's a cute place, with chalkboard signs, light-wood counters and shelving, and eight small white tables and chairs spread across the cramped dining area. Not the ideal spot for a confidential conversation. The tables are so small, only one chair fits to a side. Two girls are sitting at one of the tables. None of the other tables are occupied. There's a line, three deep of people waiting to order. The barista is a small guy in his early thirties with a light beard, glasses, and a bowtie. I never know what to think of men who wear bowties. Are they disturbed? Maybe they just crave attention. Although I desperately want a coffee, I decide to greet the girls first. They're leaning over the small table, sipping their coffee and whispering back and forth. They look up as I approach.

"Agnes? Renata? I'm Lili." They smile, but one is more enthusiastic than the other. "Can I join you?" Without waiting for an answer, I pull a chair from a neighboring table. I sit down, and the three of us huddle around a table the size of a TV tray. I turn to the one with the more enthusiastic smile. "Renata? Or Agnes?"

"I'm Agnes," she says, then points at the other girl. "That's Renata."

Renata awkwardly raises a hand. "*Szia.*"

I look back at Agnes. She has light-brown hair, and she wears it long and straight. She's thin and wears black trousers with a cute green knit top. She has long eyelashes and full lips, but something seems off about her face. I think her eyes are a little too far apart. She smiles again, and I see her teeth are overcrowded on top. I smile and turn to Renata.

I beam at her, but she doesn't match my enthusiasm. She looks down and puts her hands around the coffee cup. Renata is clearly the beauty of the two of them. Agnes is cute, but Renata is striking. She has dark, almost black hair with olive skin, a sprinkling of freckles along her nose and cheeks, long dark eyelashes, and full lips. She'd make any man stop and stare if they ran across her. No wonder she was the object of the traffickers. What I find interesting is that she's bashful. It takes her several seconds to look up again, and when she does, she flashes a fleeting smile, then looks down. Was she always this way? Or did her abduction change her?

"It's very nice to meet you both. Thank you for agreeing to see me."

Agnes looks at Renata across the table. "What do you want to know?" Agnes asks as Renata rubs a thumb on her cup, still looking down.

"I'd like to hear your story, especially Renata's."

Renata looks up at me and then back to Agnes.

"Renata really doesn't want to say anything," Agnes says.

I nod and look over at the order line. Only one woman stands at the register, and she's being served her coffee. It's torture, sitting in a coffee shop this early in the morning, smelling the rich aroma of beans all around me. "Do you girls mind if I get some coffee?"

They shake their heads, and I get up and approach the barista. He's a friendly guy, maybe too familiar. I just want coffee. I order an espresso macchiato. As he goes to work preparing it, I look back at the girls. They're whispering again, and I get an idea. After he serves me and I pay, I sit back down. I address Renata.

"I get that you'd rather not talk to me. And that's fine. Would it be okay if I ask Agnes questions about what happened to you?"

Agnes nods to Renata, and she says, "Okay." She's at least looking up now.

I smile and turn to Agnes. "I understand Renata was taken. Can you tell me what happened?"

For all the timidness Renata exudes, Agnes is the opposite. She has no trouble talking. "We went to a club, didn't we?"

Renata nods, still rubbing her finger across an imaginary scuff in the cup.

"She had met this guy, David, who convinced her to go. Well, actually, his name wasn't really David. Anyway, I didn't know about it. When we were there, I started dancing with some other guys, and Renata danced with David, or whatever his name was. Then she was just gone."

"What do you mean she was 'gone?'"

"When I turned around on the dance floor, she and David had disappeared. I searched around and couldn't find them. I went home to the apartment, and she wasn't there either."

"What did you think happened to her?"

Renata looks up and watches Agnes.

"I knew something wasn't right. Renata would never leave with a guy without telling me. I mean, she lied to me about not knowing him. But I didn't know that at the time."

Renata gives her a look.

"What? You did. I'm not saying I was perfect. I didn't tell you about Dominick."

I wonder who Dominick is, but I don't want to get too sidetracked, so I don't ask.

"So, what did you do?" I ask.

"I went to the police. I talked to this nice police guy, Peter. He helped me."

"He found Renata?"

"No." It's Renata who responds.

"Yes," Agnes says to Renata.

I smile.

"No. I escaped."

"Yeah, but who came to Ukraine and got you? Me and Peter."

Renata glares at Agnes. "The question was if Peter found me. I called you, and you and Peter came to Ukraine. But I escaped."

"Yeah, okay. But still, we came and saved you."

They both look back at me.

"How did you escape?"

Renata gets a faraway look in her eye. "They were drugging us. There was a kink in the IV in my arm, and I woke up. I was able to run away and call Agnes."

"You said *us*?"

She looks at me, and all the timidness is gone. "Yeah, there were three other girls."

I feel my excitement building. I've got her talking. "Where are they? They got away with you?"

She looks down and shakes her head.

"You left them?"

She stands from the table. Tears spring to her eyes, and she runs for the door. I look at her in shock. I turn to Agnes, but she's watching Renata run out. She stands from the table too.

"You have to understand, she feels terrible about it. About leaving the other girls there. Sorry, but I've got to go after her."

She turns and runs out, and I'm left alone in the café.

Chapter Nineteen

Peter

Peter reaches Fulton Street station and, on a whim, exits. He had planned to ride the subway to Lafayette Avenue in Brooklyn. From there, the walk would be five minutes. From here, it will be a lot more than that. But what does he care? He's got nothing else going on. This is one of his favorite parts of the city. He's right in the heart of the Financial District. Just a few short blocks away is the New York Stock Exchange. Just off Broadway is Trinity Church, where he and Karen were married. But that's not where he's going today.

He walks southeast along Fulton Street until he reaches Titanic Memorial Park. The Titanic was supposed to dock at Pier 59 in Chelsea. But, as everyone knows, it never made it. The Titanic had over twenty-two hundred passengers. Many were from New York, returning from across the Atlantic. As he crosses the park, he can see the Brooklyn Bridge, his reason for exiting the subway early. He plans to walk the bridge today, and there are two ways to enter. He can use the Brooklyn Bridge Promenade on Centre Street/Park Row or climb the staircase at Park Row Brooklyn Bridge Underpass. He chooses the promenade. It's one of his favorite views of the bridge and the city.

As he walks along the bridge, passing merchants along the way pedaling anything from art to music to jewelry, he keeps his eyes forward. It's a nice day, especially for January. The sun is high in the sky, and there isn't a cloud in sight. He's wearing a long coat, gloves, and a hat. Hats are a must for balding men on a sunshine-filled day. Like anything in life, you don't recognize the importance of something until it's gone. The lack of head hair is cold in the winter, and the sun is dangerous in the summer. You've got to protect the chrome dome.

After ten minutes of walking, Peter reaches the first suspension tower and stops. The bridge's walkway includes a white line that runs down the middle, separating pedestrians from bicyclists. Peter steps to his right around the column and looks to the east. Beneath him flows the murky waters of the East River. In the distance, he sees the skyscrapers of Manhattan, including the towers of the World Trade Center peeking over the top. Peter can remember the first time he walked along this bridge as a lonely sixteen-year-old boy. It's different now, but not vastly. Then, he had just arrived from Hungary and knew almost no English. The loneliness consumed him as he stared at the vast buildings. How could there be so many people, yet he could feel so alone? His family, with whom he never shared a closeness, remained back in Hungary. He thought of his friends. He was with them that fateful day when he was kicked out of his parents' house. He never said goodbye. He wonders if they ever learned what happened to him.

Now, he stands at the very spot he stood then. He can still remember a strange sense of calm that came to him all those years ago. Although much different than the Chain Bridge in Hungary, something about the suspension of this bridge felt familiar. Back home, they had bridges, and this similarity comforted him. Even though this new land felt like a foreign planet, there was a link. He knew someday he would learn to thrive in America.

Today, as he looks back at Manhattan, his thoughts are the same. He's alone again. Karen, the love of his life, has been taken from him. Zsuzsa, the only woman he's ever cared for beyond Karen, is back in Hungary. In a different way, she's been taken from him also. Toth threatened to kill him if he ever returned. While standing and gazing at the sun-kissed cityscape, he feels a more robust resolution within him. He relates back to that sixteen-year-old kid who was tougher than he ever knew. Peter's done hard things before, and he will again. He's going to find and bring to justice Karen's killers. And he's going to stop Toth. His jaw sets, and a line creases his forehead as he glares at the city. He spins and determinately strides along the bridge toward Brooklyn.

Thirty minutes later, he's standing outside an apartment building. He looks down at the notepad, double-checking the address. This is it. This is the address of the apartment he's seeking. He walks up the steps to the outside doors and pulls on the handle. It doesn't give way, and he frowns. He steps to the buzzer board on the wall and scans the names until he finds Kaminski. He pushes the button and waits.

After a few seconds, he hears someone say, "Hello?"

"Hello, yes, Mrs. Kaminski?"

"Yes?"

"My name is Peter. I knew your husband in the NYPD."

"My husband is gone. Please leave me alone."

He hears the disconnection of the receiver. He sighs and looks out toward the small garden surrounding the buildings. He rubs his beard and considers his options. After a minute, he pushes the button again.

The same voice answers. "Hello?"

"Ma'am, I just need five minutes of your time."

She says nothing, and he hears the receiver disconnect. Again, he sighs. He raises his head back and looks up at the overhang ceiling above him. From the corner of his eye, he sees an elderly woman approach. She's walking along the path toward him. She must be in her eighties with short white hair and a plodding gait. She's carrying a sack in her hand and having a difficult time of it. He steps down from the stairs and goes to her.

"Can I help you with that, ma'am?"

She smiles while looking up at him through her glasses. They're the kind of glasses old ladies love. The ones with a chain running from the sides and around their neck.

"Oh, my. Thank you. Going to the store is an adventure these days." She pushes the sack toward him, and he takes it. She puts a hand on his arm as she steps up the stairs. "Thank you," she says, reaching for the sack of groceries.

"I'd be happy to carry them inside for you."

Like many old ladies, she's stooped and has to press back to look into his eyes. She stands, looking him over, probably trying to determine if he's safe to let into the building. Finally, she shrugs and thanks him and gets out her key. She puts the key in the lock and enters, with Peter following.

Once they're in the elevator, he says, "I'm Peter."

They face the elevator doors, and she cranes her neck to the side and looks up at him with one eye. She's a small spitfire of a woman. "You can call me Elda Beth."

On the eighth floor, they exit the elevator, and she guides him to her door. Again, she tries to take the groceries from him, but he offers to take them in, and she agrees. When she puts the key in the lock, he hears a dog yapping. It's not anything that would cause a person to step back in fear. She swings the door open, and the dog comes bouncing out. It stops when it sees him. It's a very small, primarily orange-and-white Pomeranian.

It spins around, yapping at them while the old woman tries to calm him.

"Oh, Zorro, stop it. This is Peter."

She leans over to pick him up. She's a tiny woman, but with the stoop in her back, it seems like she's close to the ground anyway. She picks him up while the dog continues to yap. The dog climbs to her shoulder so he can watch Peter. They enter the apartment, and she points to the counter, telling him he can put the groceries down there. He complies and turns to leave when she asks if he would like anything to drink.

"I wouldn't mind some water."

She waves her hand at him, holding Zorro in the other, directing him to a chair at the small kitchen table. He sits as she walks around the counter and reaches up to get a cup out of the cupboard. She fills the cup with cold water from a pitcher she keeps in the fridge and slides it to him. She collapses into a chair across from him, seemingly exhausted. Zorro's still in her hands, and he fights to get free. The little furball hasn't stopped yapping. She sets him down, and he approaches Peter sniffing his shoes and pants. His barking subsides. Finally, after deciding Peter isn't a threat, he walks away and sits on a rug in the middle of the kitchen.

Peter takes a couple gulps of the water. "Thank you, Elda Beth."

"Would you like more?"

He does, but he doesn't want to cause her to get up to get it. "No, that's fine. Thank you."

She puts her hand flat on the table and leans toward him. "So, what's a big, handsome man like you doing hanging around our apartment building?" She winks, and he chuckles.

He considers making up a story but then decides there's little point. "I came to see someone who isn't too interested in having visitors."

"Who's that?"

"Mrs. Kaminski."

She frowns and moves her glasses off her face, letting them swing down from her neck to her chest. "How do you know Teresa?"

"I don't. Well, not really."

She gives him a curious look. "Sounds mysterious." Her spunky eyes twinkle. "Tell me."

Peter chuckles. "I was a former detective with the NYPD. I knew her husband a little."

Elda Beth says nothing, urging Peter on.

"I quit the force a year ago. I just learned her husband passed, and I had a few questions for her."

She shakes her head. "Sad situation. Man kills himself and leaves behind a wife with two children...I don't speak ill of the dead, but I never liked him, you know?"

"No?"

"No. Not a pleasant fella. They live right below me." She stomps her foot. "I could always hear him hollering at her and the kids. Some of it wasn't kind."

"Physical?"

She looks at him and nods. "That's why I don't blame her for stepping out."

Peter frowns. "Stepping out?"

"What, you think only men cheat? They have to cheat with someone."

Peter reaches up and rubs his beard. "Who with?"

"I'm not sure. I never saw the guy. But I heard him, or I should say I heard *her*. She's a screamer. She seemed to be enjoying herself. He must have been good."

Peter laughs, and Elda Beth's eyes twinkle.

"Is that still going on? Is the guy still coming around?"

"Nope. It seems to have stopped around the same time Frank died. I mean, she has some men every once in a while." She flashes a wicked smile. "But based on the noise level, they aren't the same guy."

Peter smiles and shakes his head. "I wish I could get her to talk to me."

"Why? You want to give it a try?"

Peter flushes with embarrassment. "No, not that."

She winks at him. "I know. Just kidding you. But why do you want to talk to her?"

He tells the old woman about the case he was working on, about Kaminski being dirty. He confides in her that as he was closing in, his own wife was murdered. He tells her he believes the two are related. "I need to talk to her to find out."

"I can help you. Sometimes she asks me to watch her kids when she has an errand to run and doesn't want to drag them along. I don't mind; as you can see, I don't have much happening around here. Zorro isn't great with conversation." Zorro's ears perk up at the mention of his name, and he looks at her. "Give me your number; next time she calls, I'll call you."

Chapter Twenty

Zsuzsa

I walk through the restaurant's front doors, greet the hostess, hang up my coat, and walk to the office. Kata's sitting behind the desk, reading something on the computer. I don't want to disturb her and turn to leave, but she stops me, holding up a finger.

"Have a seat. I need to talk to you."

I enter the office and sit in the chair across the desk. A sense of déjà vu hits me. Only it's a remembrance of sitting in this office with Andras instead of Kata. I hate that we still have all his old furniture. We've been so busy neither of us has made redecorating a priority, but it has to be done. The office is sparsely adorned as is, the desk, two chairs, a bookshelf with nothing on it, a couple of filing cabinets, and a solitary picture on the wall of a wolf. Its intense eyes stare at the person across the desk. Probably yet another power play by Andras. Something to intimidate and scare the person sitting across from him. Little did any of us know the wolf he was.

Kata finishes reading whatever she has on the computer, slides over, and looks at me. "How was your date?"

I can't help the smile that creeps across my face. "Nice."

She raises an eyebrow. "That's it?"

I shrug. "It was a nice night. The restaurant was beautiful, the food delicious, and the conversation informative. He had some great ideas to help us advertise the restaurant. Some of them were pretty inexpensive. One I particularly liked, he suggested we print up some simple coupons for either a free drink or appetizer and give them away with the check. People can share them with their friends and family. On the coupon, they write their name and address, and once we get them back, we mail them to the original person offering them a free appetizer or drink on their next visit. Then we note their name and address, which helps us build a mailing list."

Kata nods. "I like it. He's good."

We fall silent, lost in thought about his idea.

Kata breaks the silence. "I want to hear more about his other ideas, but right now, I want to know about the date." She's looking at me like a detective might gaze at a person of interest.

I can't help laughing as I shake my head. "What?"

"You know what."

"No, I don't."

"Yes, you do. Do you like him?"

It's the same question I've repeatedly asked myself since the date. "Oh...it's so complicated. How can I not like him? He's smart, successful."

"Gorgeous."

I laugh. "And gorgeous." I sigh. "But I'm hesitant."

"Why?"

"You know why."

"Peter." She knows how strong my feelings are for him. "That's actually what I wanted to talk to you about."

I feel my anxiety rise. Peter's never far from my thoughts, and that's been part of my hesitation with Gábor. I almost feel like I'm being unfaithful to Peter. It's stupid; we've been on one official date. We would have had a second had he not been arrested outside my apartment building. So, how can I cheat on him when I've only dated him once, and the last time I saw him, he told me he didn't have feelings for me? But he's languishing in that jail, unjustly accused of something he didn't do. And that's what makes me feel guilty.

She's peering at me, trying to read my thoughts.

"Okay," I respond, not sure what else to say.

"I heard from Peter."

"You did?"

She nods. "He called me."

A flash of irritation strikes. He can call Kata, but he can't call me? I know he was lying back in that jail when he said he didn't have feelings for me. He was protecting me. But why would he call her? Wouldn't he want to protect her too?

"What did he say?"

She hesitates and picks up a pen on the desk. She passes it from hand to hand, watching me. "Promise me you won't get mad."

I frown at her, and my look must show her I'm already there.

"At least hear me out."

I'm glaring at her, my breathing shallow and quick. "I promise."

"He's not in jail anymore."

"What? That's great! Why would I be mad at that?"

"He's not in Hungary, either...."

"Huh?"

"He went back to New York. His brother-in-law is some fancy lawyer in America who came over and got him out of jail. He wanted you to know, but he called me because he worries about putting you in danger. He thinks the person who put him in jail might come after you if he thinks Peter cares for you."

"He said this?"

"He wrote it." She opens a drawer in the desk and withdraws a paper. "He sent me an email. He told me to go to an internet café to access it. When you read it, I think you'll see why."

Kata slides the paper across the desk, and I look at her with blurry eyes. Tears spill out and run down my cheeks. I grab a box of tissues from the desk and wipe my eyes, trying to pull myself together. I sit back, holding the crumpled tissue in one hand and the paper in the other. I take a big breath, look down at the email, and read:

Kata,

I'm sorry for the abrupt phone call, but I had to get in contact with you and Zsuzsa. Please tell Zsuzsa I'm sorry for how I acted in the jail. What I said about not having feelings for her was a lie. I care for her very much. I care for both of you.

As you know, Zsuzsa and I have had a connection from the start. I was attracted to her from the moment I met her. But any association with me puts both of you in danger. The person responsible for the trafficking in the city is a powerful man. He has far-reaching connections. I have no doubt someone is watching Zsuzsa, and if I try to contact her, the result won't be good. They were listening to us in the jail. I had to make them believe I didn't care for her. I think she knew that, but please tell her. And tell her I'm sorry I never got to take her on another date.

As I told you on the phone, I'm back in New York. My brother-in-law is an attorney with the State Department of the United States and pulled some strings to get me out. I've been threatened that if I ever come back to Hungary again, I will be thrown back in jail or worse. I worry about sending this email. For your safety, I won't be contacting you again. Please understand. I hope we will one day see each other again, but I don't know when that might be.

Your Friend,

Peter

I finish reading and no longer care about the tears streaming down my face. Kata comes around the desk and wraps her arms around me. After a minute, she says, "Why don't you just go home? I'll take the night shift tonight."

I shake my head and wipe the tears with my hands. "No, I need to work. If I go home, he'll be all I can think of. Give me fifteen minutes to get myself together, and I'll be fine."

She steps back and looks at me, and I meet her eyes and force a smile. We stare at each other, then she nods and gives me one more quick hug. I walk out and go to the restroom.

Four hours later, it's 8:00 p.m., and the dinner rush is winding down. It's Csaba, the bartender's break time, and as usual, I'm filling in for him. I don't mind, especially today; I want to stay busy. Keep my mind off the heartache. My mind has drifted to Peter throughout the day, but I've forced away those thoughts by busying myself with other things. I'm not looking forward to going home tonight where I'll have to face my reflections. I walk into the kitchen to pick up an order or *töltött káposzta* (stuffed cabbage) and walk back out of the swinging door. My eyes are drawn to the man sitting at the bar. It's Gábor. I haven't seen him since our date. He notices me, and our eyes lock. I smile and wish he had come on another day. After talking with Kata, I cleaned myself up, got myself together, fixed my makeup, and got to work. But I know I'm not looking my best. There's a lifelessness to my eyes. Earlier today, one of my regulars asked if I was all right. Nothing like a question like that to make a woman feel her best.

I place the plate of *töltött káposzta* down in front of the customer, refill his beer, and make my way to Gábor.

"*Szia*," I say.

He looks at me, then says, "I'm sorry."

"Why?" I force a smile, but he can see it's fake.

He holds up his hands. "I know I was only supposed to call, but I just wanted to see you."

It's sweet, and he's adorable. But I do wish he had called. I'm not in the mood to be flirty. "It's okay. It's nice to see you too. Can I get you something to drink?"

He places his hands on the bar and studies me for a beat. "What do you have on tap?"

I rattle off a few different beers, and when I finish, he asks for a Dreher. It's the same beer Peter would always order. I look down, not wanting him to see the pain I'm feeling inside. "Coming up," I say as light and happy as I can muster. I walk to the other side of the bar and take a big breath. *Get it together, Zsuzsa. You can do this.* I grab a large mug, fill it, and give it to him. I hand him a menu and tell him I've got to check on other people, then I'll be back. I talk to a few other men at the bar and plaster a smile on my face. I can feel Gábor's eyes on me. I know he wants to talk, but I don't know what to say. I avoid him as long as I can and finally return to take his order.

"What would you like to have?"

He smiles and says, "You know, you really are the best thing about this place."

I wish he wouldn't do this. Can't he just order his food and not flirt with me? With a straight face, I say back to him, "I'm not on the menu."

His next line makes me angry when it shouldn't. He's picked the wrong night. "I wish you were. I'd order you."

My response comes out clipped, and I inwardly wince as I say it. "I don't take orders very well."

His face falls, and he's backpedaling now. "Hey, look, did I do something wrong? Do you want me to go? I know I shouldn't have dropped in unannounced."

I sigh. "It's not that. I'm sorry. I got some bad news today, and I'm just trying to get through my shift. It's not you, it's me."

He nods and looks at the menu. "How about the beef stroganoff?"

Peter's favorite. That does it. I can't keep it together any longer. I walk past the bar, down the hall, and to the office. I shut the door behind me. Tears stream down my face.

After five minutes, Csaba knocks on the door and calls through it. "Zsuzsa, I'm back from break."

I sniffle back the tears and thank him. I see the shadow of his feet under the door and know he hasn't left. He can probably hear me crying, but he doesn't ask and finally leaves. After another five minutes, I dry my eyes and give myself a pep talk. I'm not being fair to Gábor, and unless I want to push him away, I need to be nicer. I take a few deep breaths, fake a smile, and go back out there. I come around the corner expecting to see him sitting at the bar drinking his beer. Instead, his stool is empty. Gábor is gone.

Chapter Twenty-One

Detective Szabo

I sit in the shadows, looking over the dance floor. Like clockwork, here she comes again. I check my watch; she's incredibly punctual. Every fifteen minutes she does another lap around the tables asking if she can get anyone anything. Not that I'm complaining. She's a pretty woman, lean and muscular. Older than most of the kids dancing out on the club floor. I'd guess she's in her late twenties. She's wearing a short black skirt and a tight, crisp, white blouse. The top three buttons are undone. Like the last three times, she asks if I want something. I shake my head, and she walks away. She doesn't even try to hide it. She disapproves of me. I don't blame her. I've got to be the oldest person in here, and I'm drinking a club soda. Who goes to a dance club, orders a club soda, and sits at one of the tables in the back? Creeps, that's who. One of the hazards of the job. I can only imagine what she thinks.

I considered not coming. But something changes when you're the responsible party. Like a dad walking around the house turning off all the lights his kids left on. Now that's me in the task force, the one who pays the electric bill. I hate to admit it, but I have far more respect for Kovacs now. I get why he didn't let Varga be taken the last time we tried this. Every five minutes, I change my mind. I flip-flop between letting her be taken or nabbing the abductor. I know I need to let it play out, let her be abducted.

But what if we lose her? Can I live with myself, then? Sure, she's got the GPS device on her. But that could easily be removed. It's attached to the underside of her bracelet. I don't love the location, but that's the thing about women in clubs; their clothing doesn't allow for much to be hidden. We didn't have many choices. My concern is that a bracelet can quickly be taken off. Especially if she's drugged.

The club is packed with pretty women. I relax some by telling myself this plan isn't going to work anyway. What are the chances the traffickers target our plant, Officer Kocsis? From the time I saw her photo, I knew she was perfect for the role, just like Katona said. She's twenty-five, but it looks like she's eighteen. She has bright-blue eyes and long, wavy, blond hair. She's tall, maybe five foot eight. She has a beautiful smile and delicate features. What I like most about her, and why she's the perfect candidate, is her lean body. More girl than woman. That's probably why she looks like a teenager rather than a twenty-five-year-old cop.

After Katona suggested her, I ran a background check. She comes from a divorced family with one brother. She's not married and has no kids. She's from Kaposvár, a small village halfway between Lake Balaton and Pécs in southwest Hungary. Like so many other abducted women, she's not from Budapest. The chances someone knows her are remote. I called her supervisor with the Budapest police and asked if I could use her for an assignment. He agreed, and she came in to meet with me.

My first question to her was simple: "Why did you become a cop?" She gave me the company line about wanting to "serve and protect." I thought she was playing me, rehearsing a motto. I could tell from the rest of the interview that she really meant it. Her desire was sincere. She's one of those selfless people who truly cares about others. I told her about the trafficking and what we wanted her to do. There was no hesitation. She wanted to help. She approached the assignment with excitement. Not a hint of nervousness. Her focus was on the good she could do. Placing the needs of others above her own safety.

After our interview, I had little concern she could do it. Tonight's her second night on the job. She's wearing a short cocktail dress and hanging out alone, looking bored. Just as instructed. A couple of different men approached her the first night, but it never went anywhere. She danced with one or two, but it led to nothing. She's standing on the edge of the dance floor, looking like she would want to dance if asked. A man is watching her. He was here last time also. Now he goes to her. I'm too far away to hear their conversation, but I see her throw back her head and laugh, her blond hair bouncing along her shoulders. He's smiling and exudes confidence.

He's a nice-looking guy. He reminds me of Christopher Reeve in the Superman movies before his horrible horse-riding accident. He's tall, with broad shoulders. Rich, dark hair. He's wearing a button-down shirt and slacks. He buys her a drink, and they continue talking, leaning over the cocktail table. He's either hilarious, or she's an expert at playing the game. She continues to laugh over and over. Each time, she lightly touches his arm or his chest. I don't know, it looks like these two might have a genuine connection.

After a couple minutes, they move to the dance floor. They dance to several songs, if you can call it that. They bump and grind against each other, leaving little wonder about what's going on in their minds. Finally, he takes her hand and leads her off the floor. I rise from my table and follow, making sure to maintain a safe distance. I walk the dance floor's perimeter, trying to keep them in sight but not being obvious about it. He leads her down a hallway. My heart rate quickens when he pushes open an emergency door, and they enter the secluded alley. I rush forward to catch the door before it closes. Reasoning that if they hear it close, they might hear it open again. I can feel the night air as I reach the door. It's brisk, and I'm now aware of how much I've been sweating.

I hold the door open a crack, watching them walk down the alley. She's laughing at something he says. Snuggling in close to him. It's impressive. Not a hint of fear in her behavior. She knows she might be taken by a trafficker, yet she acts as if he's all that matters. In front of them sits a white Volkswagen van. The van is running, and anxiety grips me. No! I can't do this. I can't let them take her. I push the door open and lean forward, my head extending out. I prepare to break into a run, my eyes focused on the van. I can't quite make out the license plate when it happens. It's so quick, and in the blackness of night, I have no chance to react. A stick, maybe a baseball bat, comes slashing down. Pain erupts on the side of my head. I feel myself falling, but I'm not conscious long enough to brace my fall. The dim light of the alleyway evaporates.

Chapter Twenty-Two

Peter

True to her word, Elda Beth came through. She called this morning saying Teresa Kaminski had asked her to watch her kids this afternoon. She asked Peter to arrive around 2 p.m. That would ensure he is there when Teresa comes back. Now Peter sits in her kitchen, the two little kids on the couch watching SpongeBob.

"So," Elda Beth says, sitting at the table across from him. "How are you going to get Teresa to talk to you?"

It's as if she's a telepathist. He had been wondering that very thing.

"Good question. You know her; any recommendations?"

The old woman drops her glasses from her nose, letting them swing down to hang from her neck. She rubs the pink spots on either side of her nose where the glasses usually sit. "Hmm. She was married to a cop. Maybe we can play that angle. You're handsome but maybe a little old for her. Not for me, though." She winks, and he laughs.

There's a knock at the door, and Elda Beth stands and shuffles over. Before she opens it, she turns back to Peter and gives him a knowing smile. The door swings open, and a woman stands in the opening. She's young, maybe late twenties. She's not a heartstopper by any means, but she's decent looking with dark brown hair and light brown eyes. The old woman waves her inside.

"Thank you for watching them." She says to Elda Beth as she steps into the apartment. The kids remain on the couch, their eyes glued to the tv. She sees Peter and stops. "Oh, hello."

Peter stands and nods to her as Elda Beth explains. "This is my nephew, Peter. He came by just a couple of minutes ago. He loves to visit his aunt. He should do it more often." She wags a finger at him, and he smiles.

"Nice to meet you.' She says.

"You too."

Teresa walks to the kids on the couch and tells them it's time to go. They whine and lean around her, her body obstructing their view of the tv. When she tries to get them up, they beg and plead for her to let them finish the rest of the show.

"There's only a few minutes left." Elda Beth calls over to her. "Come and sit down at the table. Talk to Peter and me for a couple of minutes and let them finish."

Teresa hesitates, then gives in and comes to the table. Elda Beth offers to get her a soda, but she says she doesn't want any. Once seated, Elda Beth points at Peter.

"Peter used to be a cop."

Teresa turns her attention to him. "Oh yeah? Where? Here in Brooklyn?"

Peter shakes his head. "No, Manhattan."

"Maybe you knew my husband then, Frank Kaminski."

"Sounds familiar."

She shrugs, "He was a beat cop."

"I worked as a detective for twenty years. Started out as a beat cop."

"I told Peter about Frank." Elda Beth says, reaching across the table to pat Teresa's hand. "Terrible business." Elda Beth says to Peter. "He committed suicide, leaving her all alone with two kids to support."

"Yeah, suicide..." Teresa says, shaking her head.

"I'm sorry for your loss," Peter tells her.

She shrugs, "It wasn't all bad." Then realizing how that could sound, she explains. "I mean, there was life insurance money I didn't know he had. And he wasn't always a kind husband and father. In some ways, it's easier that he's gone."

Peter nods, and Teresa looks down at her hands. The room goes silent aside from the high-pitched nasally voice of Squidward on TV.

"I lost my wife a little over a year ago. I understand something about losing a spouse." He tells her.

She looks up from her hands. "Really? I'm sorry. Do you mind me asking how she died?"

"She was a nurse and never came home one night. Her body was found in an alleyway two days later."

"Murdered?"

Peter nods. "I think she was killed because of me."

She frowns at him. "What do you mean?"

"I think she was killed to stop me from investigating something or someone. After she died, I quit the police force. At the time, I didn't think the two were related. Now I'm sure they are."

"Who or what were you investigating?"

"Your husband." He says.

Teresa looks at him, then at Elda Beth. Fury is evident on her face. She stands from the table, walks over to the couch, and tells the kids it's time to leave. They protest, but she picks up the remote and turns the tv off. They see from her demeanor now isn't the time to protest. Elda Beth looks at Peter, shakes her head, then stands and approaches Teresa.

"Honey," Elda Beth says. "just talk to him. He doesn't want to hurt you. He just wants answers about his wife."

Teresa turns on her. "He's not really your nephew, is he? You made that up."

Without waiting for a reply, she roughly grabs each kid by the hand and walks to the door. She opens it, shepherds them both out, and shuts it behind her.

Elda Beth looks at Peter. "Why'd you go and say that?"

Peter shakes his head. "I'm not going to lie to her. If she found out, she'd never talk to me."

"She's not going to talk to you now."

He has to concede that point. He finishes the soda Elda Beth gave him, then puts the cup in the sink and tells her he might as well get going. She nods and shows him out, opening the door for him.

"Good luck with your investigation." She tells him. "I hope you get some answers."

Peter thanks her and walks down the hall. But instead of going to the elevator, he goes to the stairs and descends one level. He walks down the hall and knocks on the apartment door. After calling out to "wait a second." Teresa comes to the door. When she opens it and sees it's Peter, she tries to shut it. Peter puts his foot in the door.

"Look, Teresa. I just want to ask you a couple of questions, and I'll leave, and you'll never see me again. I need closure for my wife's murder, and I think you can help me. Just five minutes. Please?"

She stands looking at him through the crack in the opened door. Finally, she opens the door. "Five minutes."

She shows him to the table, and he sits down. The youngest, a daughter, comes to see who it is. She crawls onto her mom's lap. The boy barely looks over from the video game he's playing.

"First, I have a couple of questions for you."

"Shoot," Peter says.

"Why were you investigating my husband?"

"Because his gun was used in a murder."

"They cleared him of that, though."

"Yes, but I don't think it was a fair investigation. I was assigned the murder case; internal affairs investigated him. From the perspective of the murder, all signs pointed to him."

She nods and looks away. "Was he guilty?"

Peter shakes his head. "I don't know for sure. But I think so. Can I ask you, do you know if he was mixed up in something?"

"Like what?" She asks.

"Like drugs."

"No, he didn't take drugs."

"Did he sell them?"

She looks away and then refocuses. "I don't know. I think so. Something wasn't right. Maybe he and some other cops."

"Why do you think there were other cops involved?"

She laughs and shakes her head. "Did you ever talk to Frank?"

"No, not really."

"If you had, you wouldn't ask that. He was dumb. Stupid."

"So, you think he needed someone else? Maybe they brought him in on it. Let him take the fall?"

She nods.

"Who were the other cops?"

She shakes her head. "I'm not sure."

"Guys he worked with?"

She shrugs. "Maybe. He wouldn't say anything about it. It's just a guess. A feeling. Then after he died, two of them came here. I had never seen them before. They said he had a life insurance policy and gave me $50,000 in cash. I needed the money, so I didn't say anything. But what life insurance policy pays out in cash and sends it to coworkers to deliver? I knew something was wrong. But they're cops, you know? What was I supposed to do? So, I took the money and kept my mouth shut."

"Can you tell me anything about the cops that brought the money?"

"I can tell you the names they gave me. But you didn't hear any of this from me. If anyone asks, I'll deny it." She looks down at the little girl she's holding. "I've got kids. You know?"

Peter nods. "Agreed."

"Chief of Special Operations O'Hare and Detective Caruso."

Chapter Twenty-Three

Director Toth

I walk out of my office building, unlock my door, and slide into the rich black leather seat of my Mercedes Benz S Class. I grip the steering wheel, put the automobile in reverse, and back out of my parking space. With a flick of my wrist, I pull out my sunglasses and put them on while accelerating out from the underground parking garage. I turn right and travel a couple blocks until a red light stops me. A young couple stands on the side of the road, waiting to cross. The man points to my car, saying something to the girl. He's trying to see in through the window. People are always curious about who's inside. It's just another reason I love this car. Not only does it handle like a blade through soft butter, but it also attracts attention. Jealousy. He's telling her how he'll have a car like this someday. "Stick with me, babe. That'll be me someday."

The light turns green, and I fire off the line like a sprinter coming out of the blocks. I watch in my rearview mirror as their gaze follows me. The sun is high in the sky, and it's a nice, moderately warm day for January. What little snow remains has been painted gray with dirt and sand. I come up a slight rise, and the buildings fade from sight as I drive along the Margit Bridge. When I reach the midway point, I look to my left and notice the railing has already been replaced. That was the spot where Detective Kovacs, former task-force leader, had met his untimely demise. I look back to the road and shake my head. *Such a shame.*

I hit some traffic as I reach the Buda side of the city. It's always congested over here. Even at midday, like now. Typically, this traffic would make my blood boil. But not today. Today my thoughts are consumed by my impending meeting. It has to go well. It has to. There's no other option. I need to play this delicately. I've rehearsed it over and over in my mind.

I ascend the hill and reach the gates to the Castle District. The guards stop me, and I tell them who I am and why I'm here. They wave me through. I hear the rumble of the tires on the cobblestone street as I climb the hill. I turn right and head toward the castle, bumping along the uneven road. A line of Hungarian flags flies to my right. I reach the castle, but that's not my destination. I turn and park in a reserved space in front of the Sándor Palace, home of the president of the Republic of Hungary. After I'm stopped, I pull out my briefcase, make sure my suit and tie are in place, and stride toward the front door. A green guard shack stands on either side of the large green doors, and one of the guards comes forward. He bows and asks my business. I tell him I have an appointment with the president. He asks for my name and refers to his sheet on a clipboard before nodding and telling me I can enter. I push through the green doors and am greeted by a man who seems to be expecting me.

"Director, thank you for coming," he says as he extends his hand. He's a small man with a gentle touch. He's dressed in a suit and tie. He's always made me feel welcome when I've come, and I can see why he has risen to the role of Secretary to the President. He shows me down a hall and up a flight of stairs until we reach the president's office. He asks me to sit while he confirms President Mádl is ready to see me.

After I wait for a few minutes, he comes back and bids me to enter. I walk through the doors, and President Mádl stands at the side of his desk, a large smile on his face. He steps forward, extending his hand to me. "Welcome."

I take it and look him in the eye. I'm about five inches taller than he is, and I'm forced to bow my head to see him better. He's a born politician. If I didn't know better, I'd think the man adores me. His greeting is so warm and inviting. He asks me to sit, and I seat myself in the chair across from his desk. He waits, then walks around and settles in his chair.

Once he's situated, he gets down to business. He opens a file on his desk, and the smile vanishes. "I really appreciate you coming in today, Director." He says this without looking up. His glasses are now perched on the end of his nose. He reads aloud statistic after statistic of the country's crime levels over the last year, comparing it to the prior. Almost all are trending in the right direction. The country is safer. He then starts comparing those percentages and levels to our neighboring countries. Again, our record is stellar in most categories. "I must say, Director, you've done well in so many areas. How have you done it?"

Like any good leader, I give praise to my team. I tell him how I couldn't do it without them. That I'm surrounded by great people. He nods and sits back in his seat, steepling his hands and resting his elbows on the arms of the chair. Here comes the bomb. "So why are they failing you when it comes to abductions? Especially when young teen girls are concerned?"

He's staring at me now, and I know the pleasant part of the meeting is over. This is it, and I'm ready.

"Sir, as you know, abductions and missing-persons cases are growing everywhere across Europe. Not just in Hungary. It's a problem every nation faces. None seem to be able to identify why. But, I can guarantee you, that area is at the top of my objective list for 2001. We must make improvements, and we will."

He takes a large breath, leans back, and rubs his forehead. "And how do you plan to do that?"

"I've successfully lowered crime levels in many areas by aggression. I don't hide from a problem. I face it head-on. For example..." I tell him about the undercover officer who was recently abducted. About how we've allowed her to be taken rather than arrest the perpetrators so we can track their movements and learn their patterns. "I know it's dangerous. And I know we might lose an agent or two. But by being more aggressive, we'll be able to find the root of the problem."

He takes another large breath and rubs his chin. "And how long will that take?"

I look him in the eye and know this is the time. I'm prepared for this. "Before I answer that, can I ask you a question?" He nods, and I remain still, my back not touching the cushion behind me. "Do I have your support?"

He looks at me, and any warmth I saw before is gone. "No."

I'm a little surprised. But I don't show it. I thought he'd dance the political dance. The same one politicians do across the world. Although it's not the answer I want, I respect his candor. "Why not?"

He leans forward and points to something in the file. "Because over the last three years, the rate of abductions remains high. You see the same numbers I do. Knowing that, I ask myself why you haven't fixed it. Maybe you've tried but you can't. Why should I believe it will be different now?"

I know exactly what I'm going to say to this. "As I told you before, the abduction rate is number one on my priority list this year. It's never been number one before. Murder has. Corporate fraud. You can see how those crimes have dropped since 1999. This is now number one for me. And I pledge to you the same success."

He looks me in the eye while nodding. I can see I've reached him. "József, my biggest problem is the media. Two years ago, even last year, they weren't reporting this stuff. Now they badger me with it. If I stop getting asked about this, you'll have my support."

We stare at each other, an understanding in our eyes.

Later that night, after dinner, I excuse myself as my daughter sits at the dining table and works on her homework, and my wife does the dishes. I walk to my office door, open it, and shut it behind me. I sit at my desk and dial. After a single ring, the voice greets me.

"Hello, sir."

"What did the reporter say?"

A pause. "He wouldn't go for it."

"Nothing?" I growl.

"Nothing. I increased the bribe three times. He wouldn't change his mind. Gave me some crap sermon about ethics. He's going forward with the story."

"How soon?"

"In two days."

I can feel my chest rising and falling. My teeth gritted. "I'll take it from here."

"I can do it, Boss."

I shake my head. "No. I'll do it myself."

Chapter Twenty-Four

Lili

I reach the sixth floor of the apartment building, check my notes, and knock. As I stand waiting, staring at the scuffed white door, I listen for any movement. From within, my knock has brought no audible creaking of floors or shuffling of feet. No interruptions in conversation. Two other doors are on this side of the stairwell. One has decorations all around it. A pot with fake flowers, a welcome mat, and a neatly stenciled quote beneath the peephole. The other is plain. The door looks like it's never been painted. It's brown with smudges and cracks all over. I knock again and wait. This time, I can swear I hear something. It's faint, but it sounds like a light shuffle of feet. I stare into the peephole, smile, and wave.

"Agnes? Renata? I know at least one of you is home. Come on, talk to me."

Nothing.

I bang on the door now. A dog starts barking. It's more of a fierce grumble. It's probably one of those dogs that are as big as a horse and have a face that terrifies small children. And me. *Please don't let that door open and it's a little old lady trying to hold it back from devouring me.* On my other side, I hear a door open. A woman peers out through the crack in it. Seeing I'm not threatening, she opens the door wider. She's middle-aged. She's wearing a pink sweater and black pants with pink house slippers.

I turn to her. "Do you know the girls who live here?" I point to Agnes and Renata's door.

"I do."

I put my hand on my hip and do my best exasperated look. "I've been trying to reach them. They won a contest through our television station a few days ago."

I pull out my business card and show it to her. She takes it from me and smiles.

"Well, how nice is that? What'd they win?"

I blurt out the only thing I can think of. "Well, a TV, of course. Big and beautiful. Very expensive."

She smiles and points at me. "You look familiar. Are you the 'Shopping Queen?'"

This is the first time anyone has recognized me from TV, and it's probably the last place I would ever expect it.

"Guilty," I say.

"Oh, my, I just love your segments. I love to shop."

"Well, of course. You're a woman, aren't you? Don't we all?"

We both laugh, and she shakes her head. "What a day. I never thought I'd meet someone famous today." She turns back to their door. "They're home. They're just a little scared. Let me try." She walks over to the door while I step back. She knocks on it and calls, "Agnes. Renata. It's Agi. There's a nice girl here from on the TV. Open up."

She turns around and smiles, and I smile back. After a few seconds, the door opens, and Agnes is standing there in a pair of pajama pants and a T-shirt. Her hair is up, and she's not wearing any makeup. "Sorry, I'm not feeling too good."

Agi goes to her, putting her hand on her forehead. "Oh, dear. Are you sick?"

"I think so."

Agi turns around and looks at me. "Well, this might be why you've had a hard time reaching them." She turns back to Agnes. "This pretty young lady is from the TV. You've won yourself a new one."

Agnes looks at me, and our eyes lock. She looks back at her neighbor, forcing a grin. "Okay, then. I'll invite her in."

Agi looks at me, smiles like she's just fixed the world's problems, and gestures for me to enter the apartment. I thank her, step inside the door, and shut it behind me. Agnes and I stare at each other in the cramped entrance.

"I've been calling you for two days. You don't answer your phone or your messages."

Agnes stands with her arms folded; a bratty-little-sister's look on her face. "You weren't calling me. You were calling Renata."

I roll my eyes. "I was calling both of you."

"Well, you should have said so. Sounded to me like you only wanted to talk to her, and she doesn't want to talk to you."

"Is she here?"

She shakes her head. "She's at school."

"Shouldn't you be at work?"

She flips her head at me. "No...Mom. I'm off today."

This isn't going well. I need her on my side. I need to be her friend, not her older sister. "I'm sorry. Are you really sick?"

She shrugs. "I'm just tired. You want to sit down?"

She leads me into the kitchen. Against the wall, there's a small square table with chairs on opposite sides. She plops down in one, and I take the one opposite.

"I don't think Renata is going to talk to you. You might as well stop trying."

I watch her, reading her eyes. "What about you?"

"What about me?"

"Will you talk to me?"

She narrows her gaze. "About what?"

"About what happened to Renata. And your part in it."

She scrunches up her face and points at herself. "What do you mean *my part*?"

"I mean that you're her best friend. I want to know how it impacted you."

"Oh," she says, standing up quickly as if she's forgotten something. "Did you want some water or something?"

I smile and shake my head. Her adolescence is showing through. It's like her mother taught her how to treat guests, and she hasn't done it and will be in trouble. "No, I'm fine. I just want to talk to you."

She exhales and plops back down on the chair. "Something did happen to me too, you know?"

I didn't. "No, tell me about it."

"They tried to take me also. But I got away. I fought off my attacker. Right here in this room."

My excitement shoots through the roof. Things just got a lot more interesting. Maybe I don't need to talk to Renata after all.

"Tell me. Tell me everything."

Chapter Twenty-Five

Peter

Peter gets off the bus at Lexington Avenue and Fifty-Second Street. The Seventeenth Precinct, the place he felt he belonged most, is just around the corner. For twenty years, this was his professional home base. Now, looking back, he realizes it meant more to him than anything other than Karen. There, he was like Norm at Cheers. When he walked in, everyone would call out his name. But right now, he's doing his best to stay out of sight. At least until he gets in the building. He circles the block, heading down Lexington, then up Fiftieth Street, and enters Ess-a-Bagel. It's a place he knows well. He used to come here a couple times a month. He knows exactly where he wants to sit. He orders tea and sits at the bar facing the exterior windows. He picks a seat pointing toward the police station. From this vantage point, he can see his old partner's parking spot and the front doors of the precinct.

For the last twelve hours, since talking to Teresa, he's gone back and forth between doubting and believing what he heard from her. He still can't believe his friend and former partner was involved in the plot to kill his wife. They were together almost every day for four years. He and Karen had been there when Tony's kids were baptized. Tony had been in his and Karen's home numerous times. How could someone do that? Peter had seen enough murder in his life to understand how horrible human beings can be to each other. But those people were strangers. His friends, his partners, couldn't be like that. Could they?

The evidence is stacked against it, but Peter still holds out hope. Maybe Tony was told to sign off on Kaminski's investigation without going to the crime scene. Perhaps the other man with him at Teresa's home forced him to go along. But even as Peter thinks it, he knows he's being naïve. He saw Tony's look when he asked for the widow's address. He knows him too well. He knows the truth. Today he'll confirm his suspicions.

Peter remains diligent, watching the parking space and the front door. The parking space remains occupied. The vehicle is a Chevy Malibu. Newer than the one Tony drove when they were partners. Peter watches former coworkers and friends file in and out of the building for thirty minutes. Finally, the wait pays off. Tony appears. He says something to Hamby, a cop standing out front smoking a cigarette, walks to his car, and drives away.

Peter takes this as his cue. He walks out of the bagel shop, crosses the street, and enters the precinct. Janet's on the phone, like always, and doesn't notice him. People rarely react when things look normal. We're trained to pay attention to the unexpected. Peter acts like he belongs here. He walks past her and heads down the hallway. He knows his timing is perfect. Most of the detectives are out of the office following leads. He walks through the room of cubicles, down the hall, and stops at the door with the name of Lieutenant Bridges on the outside. He can hear Bridges on the phone. From the tone of the conversation, he's talking with his wife. Peter knocks and opens the door. Bridges is leaning over his desk, forehead in his hands, elbows on the wood.

He looks up, surprise in his eyes. "Peter?" he mouths. Peter smiles and waves and sits down in the chair opposite the desk.

"Listen, Linda, I've got to go. Something came up. You'll have to yell at me when I get home."

Peter can hear her still talking into the phone as Bridges hangs up.

"Linda," he says, rolling his eyes. He leans back in his chair. "It's so good to see you. I'm glad you came back. I heard you came in the other day. Why didn't you let me know you were coming? I was sorry I missed you."

"Yeah, sorry about that. It wasn't planned; I was in the area and decided to pop in. I was disappointed not to see you. I had to come back."

"I'm glad you did. How are you?"

Peter and Lieutenant Bridges came up together in the ranks. They went through training together and were both "rookies" at the same time. After Peter became a detective and moved to Special Investigations, they worked less together but remained good friends. Bridges was the one nominated to tell him about Karen's death.

"Not bad. Doing better. I've been away for a while and thought it would be fun to come back and visit."

Bridges nods, but there's a crease on his forehead, and the skin around his eyes wrinkles. "How's it been over there? Therapeutic?"

Peter shrugs. "It's a lot different than when I was a kid. I barely recognized the place. My Hungarian also needed some practice." Peter chuckles. "But I'm getting up to speed."

"I bet." Bridges chuckles. "I mean, I don't know how to speak any languages. But I can imagine not speaking for that long would do that to someone."

For the next fifteen minutes, they catch up. Bridges tells him about his family. His kids are teenagers and deciding on a college. He's thinking about retiring from the force after another few years.

"How is it?" Bridges asks.

"How's what?"

"Not being in this place every day. Do you miss it? Or is it wonderful? It's wonderful, right?"

Peter laughs. "I miss some of the people, like you. But I don't miss the bureaucracy and the pressure. I control my schedule and can choose the cases I work on now. I like that." Peter leans forward. "Speaking of, there's something I've been wondering about."

"Shoot."

"There was a case I was investigating. A murder had taken place during a drug deal, and a cop's gun had been used as the murder weapon. The cop's name was Frank Kaminski. Ring any bells?"

Bridges nods, a faraway look in his eye like he's trying to remember the specifics. "Right, I remember that." His eyes focus as he looks at Peter. "Kaminski is dead. Committed suicide. Shocked the whole department."

"Wow," Peter says, acting surprised.

"Yeah. Sad situation. He had two young kids."

"Are you sure it was suicide?"

Bridges was looking up at the ceiling, remembering the time. Hearing this, he snaps his head down to look at Peter. "You think it might have been something else?"

Peter holds up his hands. "Oh, I don't know. I just wanted to make sure they investigated it. Something didn't sit right with me on the gun situation. He claimed to have had the gun stolen, but I'm not convinced."

Bridges chews his lower lip. "Hmm. Hang tight. Let me go pull the file."

He leaves, and Peter smirks. After five minutes, he returns with the file. He sits down next to Peter and opens it. Then, as if thinking of something, he closes it and looks at Peter. "You're a civilian now. I really shouldn't be showing you this."

Peter looks away. "Oh, sorry. I don't want to get you in trouble."

Bridges waves a hand. "Oh, who am I kidding. You aren't a civilian, even if you don't carry a badge anymore. We'll just keep it our little secret." He reopens the file, and they lean over and start reading.

Thirty minutes later Peter walks out of the precinct. As he heads down Fifty-Second Street, avoiding the heavy foot traffic, his mind spins with the implications of what he just saw. Most people wouldn't have noticed it. It was a photocopy of the suicide note. The note was typed, which is odd, unless the suicide was planned. Rarely do people who commit suicide type a note. It's typically a handwritten message produced right before the act. But it wasn't even that which grabbed his attention. It was one word in the note. Peter had seen multiple reports and messages written by Kaminski during his investigation. Kaminski didn't know the correct usage of "they're." He would repeatedly misuse the term opting for "their." One line in the suicide note read, *I hope they're okay.*

It referred to his wife and kids. Prior to Peter going inside the precinct, he doubted Kaminski took his own life. Now, he's positive he didn't. So, who wrote the note? And who killed him? Whoever did, Peter's sure, acted to cover their own guilt.

Chapter Twenty-Six

Zsuzsa

I walk in the big glass doors, and I'm stopped by a security guard. He's not the same one who stopped me when I was here last. This guy is big with a red, scruffy beard and glasses. He looks like he's mad at the world. He barely opens his mouth when he asks what business I have. I tell him I'm here to see Detective Szabo.

"Have an appointment?"

I say I don't but give my name and explain that Szabo will want to see me. He looks me up and down, and I guess at his thoughts. I'm wearing a long coat with no skin visible, yet men still do this to me. I'm not surprised I get leering glances when wearing tight-fitting clothing. But a long winter coat? Really? What are they hoping to see? I shiver as he looks at me. After he's through with his daydream, he asks me to wait while he calls on the phone. I hear him ask for Detective Szabo. I was right. Szabo does want to see me. He nods and says, "Yes, sir." He comes back over, walks me through the metal detectors, then asks me to sit and wait. I pick the same seat as the last two times, cross my legs, and stare out the window. I barely have a chance to look around when I hear Szabo. The big man is thumping down the stairs, belly propelling him forward. He sees me, smiles, and waves. Oh, how much more pleasant he is now than before.

When he reaches me, he extends his hand, and I reluctantly take it, remembering the last time. "I'm surprised to see you. Peter isn't here anymore."

I nod as I wipe my hand on my coat. "I know."

He stares at me, and I stare back, our faces expressionless.

He turns away from me and looks out the glass doors. "How about a walk?"

"I'd love one."

I really wouldn't. But I let him take me by the elbow and lead me past the guards and out through the doors. The sun is shining, but it's cold. I'm glad I have my coat and gloves. After we've walked several paces, I look up at him.

"Why did you arrest Peter?"

He looks at me, then back in front of him. We're walking on the sidewalk in a busy part of the city. Cars, trucks, and buses zoom past. He's so tall I wonder if he heard me. After a pause, I get my answer.

"Because all the evidence pointed toward him for the murder of Detective Kovacs. And because we had nothing else. No other leads."

"How can you say that? He was standing next to Kovacs on the bridge. You knew he wasn't driving."

"Yes, but we thought it was his idea. He had an accomplice. Or maybe he paid someone to do it." He shakes his head. "I know. I can see how, on the outside, it seems like a stretch. But there was more."

"Like what?"

"I can't tell you that."

We have to wait for a light to turn before crossing the street. People are around us, so I wait to ask my next question. Once we're moving again and have some distance, I ask, "So why did you let him go?"

He lets out a big sigh and pauses. "He has powerful friends in the United States. Politically, there's no way we could have held him any longer."

He's telling me the truth. That's what Peter said in his email.

"Is that the only reason you let him out?"

He stops and looks at me. He's trying to read my thoughts. Maybe trying to see if there's a hidden meaning to my question. "Why do you ask?"

"I want to know if you still think he's guilty."

He stares at me and chews on his inner cheek. "No, I don't think he's guilty."

"What changed?"

"I can't tell you everything, but I can say we searched his apartment, his office, everywhere. We couldn't find any evidence to tie him to the driver. I don't think Peter's involved."

I nod. "Should we head back?"

He agrees, but before we move, I decide to trust him.

"Peter told me there was a girl abducted in Újpest. Someone who didn't fit the mold. He said she was the key to determining who was instigating the trafficking. Have you looked into that? Did you find the girl?"

"We found the girl."

"And?"

"She's dead."

I stop and look at him. I can feel my face drained of color. "They killed her? Why?"

He sighs and shakes his head. "I'm not sure. I tried to talk to the mother, but she wouldn't say anything. She knows something, but she's scared. I don't blame her."

We begin walking again as I process this. Did Peter know this was going to happen?

"Let me talk to the mother."

He looks at me and shakes his head.

"She won't talk to you because you're a big, scary detective. I'm a nobody. Let me speak to her woman to woman. Maybe she'll open up."

He stops walking again, and I can see he's considering it.

"I'll be careful. Whatever I learn, I'll report back to you."

He stares at me and finally nods. "Okay. I'll get you her name and address."

An hour later, I walk into the restaurant for my shift. Kata's waiting for me at the entrance. She's already got her coat and purse.

"I've got to run. Sorry, I can't stay and chat. There's something for you in the office." She winks and smiles and walks out.

After putting up my coat, I walk to the office and see a vase with a dozen red roses. I pick up the one-line note next to it. It reads, *I'm sorry.* I turn the message over, but there's no signature.

Chapter
Twenty-Seven

Detective Szabo

A knock on the door causes me to jump and close the window on my computer screen. I turn away and face the entrance to my office.

"Come in."

Arpad, our IT specialist, opens the door. My heart rate accelerates. *Did he see what I was looking at?*

"How can I help you, Arpad?"

He doesn't immediately answer. Instead, he steps into my office and shuts the door. A prickle of sweat rolls down my back.

"You asked me to tell you if the GPS device came back online."

The GPS device we had on the girl taken in the club hadn't worked since five minutes into the abduction. We've been trying for days to bring it back online with no luck. Over the last day, any hope we had was extinguished. Guilt replaced it. I haven't been able to sleep as I think about what that girl may be going through. The idea that we might have a glimmer of hope is more than I can imagine. My excitement is evident in my reply.

"Yes. It's on? You've got something?"

He holds up his hands in wonder. "It came back on a few minutes ago."

"Where is she?"

He walks around my desk and places a printout in front of me. It's a map with a red dot. The red dot indicates Celja. I look back up at him.

"Where's that?"

"Slovenia."

A new country. Andras had been taking the girls to Zagreb in Croatia. Csaba, the nightclub manager, was using Kyiv in Ukraine. Now we've got someone else using Celja in Slovenia. All neighboring countries to Hungary.

I rise from my desk, startling Arpad. "Thank you. I need this." I pick up the sheet and head for the door. I walk through the bullpen area as several members of my team look up at me with curiosity. I continue down the hall and pull up outside Toth's office. I knock and wait. I hear voices inside, and the conversation stops.

"Yes?" The sound is muffled, but I can tell it's the director.

I call through the door, "Director, I need to talk to you. It's urgent."

"Come in."

I open the door and see Detective Katona standing in the room across the desk from the director. I look at him, then at Toth. The surprise I'm feeling must show on my face. Toth flicks a wrist at Katona and points to the door. He nods and walks past me, not looking at me. He shuts the door, and I look at Toth for an explanation.

"A complaint has been lodged against Detective Katona from his time with the city police. I had some questions for him."

I say nothing, just stare at him, then I remember why I came. I raise the sheet in my hand and walk toward his desk.

"The GPS device planted with Officer Kocsis has come back online." I slide the paper on the desk in front of him. "She's in Slovenia. I'd like to go check it out."

He looks down at the paper, then back up at me. "And do what?"

"What do you mean?"

He cocks his head to the side. "I mean, Detective, and do *what*? Stake out the location? Or go in guns blazing?"

I hadn't really thought about that. When we conceived this plan, we were going to follow Kocsis. See where they took her. See who the players were. That might still be a possibility.

"I guess I'd like to stake it out. See if we can learn anything."

He nods and looks back down at the paper. "When it crosses our borders, I have to involve Interpol. I'll need to give Slovenia a heads-up too." I can see why he wants to do this, but I'd like to keep it as quiet as possible. "Go ahead and go. Take most of your team with you and Arpad so you can track the GPS in real time. Leave one member of your team behind."

"Yes, sir." I head for the door.

"Which team members are you taking?"

I turn around and look at him. "Varga and Farkas. They've been on the team the longest."

He shakes his head. "No, take Farkas and Katona. Leave Varga here."

I frown, but he waves his hand, picks up the paper, and studies it. I walk out and shut the door. As I head down the hallway, I notice Katona is waiting for me. I can't help the frustration I feel as I look at him. Shouldn't Toth have told me Katona had a complaint against him? Isn't he a member of my team? And why is Toth telling me who I can take to Slovenia?

"Sir, I know how that must have looked. He called me in. I didn't—"

"I don't care. Come on, we're going to Slovenia. Let's go tell the rest of the team."

Chapter Twenty-Eight

Peter

Peter exits the subway and walks up the steps at the Fifty-Ninth and Lexington station. It's the closest to Gary and Becky's spacious apartment in Midtown East. After living with Karen for so long, Peter dreaded coming home to a lonely apartment. Although he likes people on a case-by-case basis, he would never consider himself a social butterfly. But after living on his own for over a year, he can see that maybe he enjoys company more than he thought. Last night, when he arrived in the apartment, Gary and Becky were sitting on the couch drinking wine and watching TV. They were cuddled up like two teenagers. Rachel was in her room listening to music on her Discman. Headphones on. He couldn't see her, but he could hear her through the door when he walked to the spare bedroom. She was singing her favorite song, "Oops… I Did It Again," at the top of her lungs. Good thing the girl is so intelligent; she doesn't have a future in singing.

The scene did something for him. For the first time in over a year, he felt part of a group. He had a family. This time in New York has been precisely what he needed. It's done wonders for his soul. His only concern is taking advantage of their hospitality. How long should he stay before he finds a place of his own? He nears the building, and as he comes around the corner, he sees a stocky figure milling around the entrance under the canopy. He considers turning around and coming back later. But curiosity, as much as anything, propels him forward. As he nears the entrance, his former partner Tony sees him approach. Peter stops in front of him and looks down on him, trying to contain the loathing he feels. He knows he needs to control his emotions and think clearly. The man was involved in the murder of his wife.

They nod to each other, and Tony speaks first.

"Heard you were at the station today."

Peter's curious why he would say it straight out. He's not surprised he knows; he saw several people on his way out, not to mention the time he spent with Bridges. Plus, cameras are everywhere in there. But why wouldn't Tony try to hide the knowledge?

"I was. Bridges wasn't there the other day when I stopped by. I wanted to see him."

Tony nods. He has his hands in his coat pockets and looks down at his scuffed shoe. He kicks at a cigarette butt on the sidewalk. "Nothing else?"

"What do you mean?"

He's been rocking back and forth and stops, looking up at Peter with one eye. His face is in profile. "You're not investigating something?"

Peter sees little advantage in responding to this.

"Look, Peter, I'm here as a friend. Whatever you're doing, stop it. Just leave it alone. Go back to Hungary and forget all this."

It's the word *friend* that starts Peter's blood boiling. He can't help himself. "Friends don't kill other friends' wives."

Tony takes his hands out of his pockets and squares up. "I'm warning you."

"No, I'm warning you, Tony. Come clean now. Maybe you get a deal. Use the others as leverage. Maybe the DA goes easy on you. You'll do some time, but you might have a life again someday. But mark my words, I'll find out what happened and expose it. I won't rest."

Tony looks at him, and Peter can see an equal anger in his eyes.

"Just remember, Peter, I tried to warn you."

He steps off the curb and walks away.

Chapter Twenty-Nine

Director Toth

I considered killing him at his home. But he has a dog, a wife, and two kids. The coordination of that is too complex. Plus, the likelihood of something going wrong and me needing to kill another person was too great. His wife and kids didn't do anything. They don't deserve to die.

I thought about the newsroom, but again, too many uncontrolled possibilities. That's when I came up with this plan. It's perfect and more accessible than I thought. It started with a fake email account. That took five minutes. The inconvenient part was finding an internet café to go to. I didn't want to use my office computer. I'm not sure what our IT department can and can't track. Better to be safe. To bait the hook, I started by being unsure and tentative. I wrote an email that went like this:

Dear Mr. Halasz,

A friend of mine showed me your article about the missing girl from Pápa. Finally, someone is talking about this. My daughter went missing last year, and nobody, including the police, seemed to care. I have some information I can share with you.

Sincerely,

Concerned Citizen

He responded in an hour, but I didn't see it until I returned to the internet café the next day.

Concerned Citizen,

Thank you for your email. It seems this problem is even more significant than I knew. I'd love to talk to you. My phone number is at the bottom of this email. Call me anytime.

All the best,

Halasz Béla

I responded immediately:

Dear Mr. Halasz,

I can't call you on the phone for reasons I can't explain here. I'll only give you this information in person. Contacting you at all is a risk. I could be putting my family in further danger, and I need to know I can trust you.

Sincerely,

Concerned Citizen

I ran an errand and came back to the café an hour later.

Concerned Citizen,

Come to our news offices. Whatever you tell me, I will hold in confidence. I won't reveal you as my source. If you don't feel comfortable coming here, I can go to you. Just tell me when and where.

All the best,

Halasz Béla

I smiled as I read it. He had swallowed the bait. All I needed was to reel in the line.

Dear Mr. Halasz,

Meet me tonight at 9 p.m. I'll be on Margit Island at the southern tip under the bridge. There's a small children's park there. Come alone. If I see you have anyone with you, I'll leave and know I can't trust you. Tell no one you're coming. I can't risk the exposure.

Sincerely,

Concerned Citizen

I arrive on the island an hour early. Just as I assumed, the island is deserted. It's January, and although unseasonably warm, the sun goes down at five this time of year. Nobody's playing in a park three hours after the sun has gone down. I park in the middle of the island, far away from our designated meeting spot. I walk around to the back and pull out the chains, wrapping them around my shoulders to best carry them. The jaunt is only about a half mile, but it leaves me winded, and my calves, quads, and shoulders burn from the strain. I stash the chains under the big tree at the point of the island. I look back to make sure they're positioned out of view.

I once used this spot for a similar meeting. This time the result will be far different. He had his chance. Now, he's going to die. I walk back near the base of the staircase leading down from the bridge. The island is accessible in two ways. Either you walk down the steps from the Margit Bridge, or you drive onto the island, like I did. The steps are a more common method and more convenient. Driving can be difficult, especially if you aren't familiar with the route. From this vantage point, I can see him coming down the stairs. And, if he decides to drive, he can only get so far. Eventually, he'll need to park and walk, which will take him right past me. I hunch in the shadows and wait.

After several minutes, I see someone descending the stairs. Actually, I hear him more than I see him. His feet are heavy, and he has a tendency to shuffle as he walks. He descends the stairs, turns to his left, and makes his way to the point of the island and the park. I begin to follow, maintaining a distance of at least thirty feet. He reaches the park and stops at the large children's play toy.

"Hello?" he calls out. "Anyone here?"

I look behind him in each direction. He's come alone, just as instructed. A bench sits to the side of the park, and he goes to it and sits down. I creep around behind him. I grip the tool in my hand. He sits looking out at the river, the city lights in front of him, but the park is engulfed in shadows. When I get within a few feet, a twig snaps under my foot. He spins around, and I close the remaining distance thrusting my tool into his chest. A chorus of snapping sounds and bright lights emanate from him. His body goes rigid, and he slumps to the ground. I fish my gloved hand into my pocket and pull out a set of handcuffs. I turn him over and fasten them to his wrists. I turn him back and put my knee into his sternum. I can see he's looking at me but unable to talk. All he can do is grunt and labor as he sucks in air.

"Thanks for meeting me, Béla," I whisper. I don't really need to whisper, but why push my luck. My genius is my preparation. I planned everything. Even the poetic justice of his last name and method of death. "I have a few questions I want to ask you. You aren't going to speak. Instead, you'll blink. One blink for 'yes' and two blinks for 'no.' Should you decide to try and scream, I slit your throat, and you bleed to death right here. Understand?"

He looks at me, registers the conversation has begun, and blinks once.

"Good. Did anyone else know you were coming here tonight?"

He blinks twice. I stare into his face and press my knee further into his sternum. He closes his eyes in pain.

"I think you're lying to me. Did you tell someone you work with?"

He blinks twice.

"Your wife?"

He blinks twice again. I push my knee still further into his sternum. He gasps in pain. I release some pressure.

"You didn't tell anyone?"

He blinks once.

I nod. "Good." I let him take a couple deeper breaths before applying the pressure again. I'm not cruel. "Do you have another article coming out about the abductions?"

He blinks once.

"Will it run tomorrow?"

He blinks twice.

"This week?"

He blinks once.

I nod and lean forward, pressing the taser into his shoulder. His body goes rigid as the tool jumps in my hand. He says nothing, and tears begin to stream out of his eyes.

"Don't worry. I won't tase you again."

I grab him by the shoulders and drag him twenty feet to the waterfront. I leave him handcuffed and motionless at the edge of the cold water. I walk back to the large tree, gather the chains, and return with them slung over my shoulders. I wrap the chains around his body, starting from the shoulders and moving down to his feet. Once I've secured him, I pull out a padlock and lock the chain together.

He's grunting now, trying to plead but unable to form the words. I look him in the face and say, "You should have taken the money." I step past him into the water. It's so cold it makes me gasp. I grasp the chain around his shoulders and drag him into the water. He's trying to fight but can only manage a slight wiggle. His eyes are wide as his face becomes submerged in the muddy water. I wade deeper and deeper until the current makes me feel unstable. His legs are twitching more now. He's fighting me. I walk back around, grab his legs, and push him deeper into the water. His legs go still, and I know he's lost consciousness. I push and roll his body until I'm sure he won't be visible from the shore. Likely, his body will drift deeper and deeper into the river over time. He'll never be found.

I exit the water and retrace my steps, ensuring nothing is left behind. Then I walk to my car. When I reach it, I pop the trunk, change my clothes, and get behind the wheel. I start the car, pull out, and turn on the heat. I wish I hadn't needed to get my feet and hands so cold. I could have shot him. But where's the creativity in that? Plus, I don't like a mess. This plan is genius, and it makes me smile. How many people would kill a man with the last name of 'Fisher' by drowning him in a river? At the exact location people often fish? The thought warms my cold limbs and makes it all worth it.

Chapter Thirty

Lili

Anna gives me a look when I pass her approaching my desk. I know I'm late again. I don't need her to point it out. I put down my purse, take off my coat, then boot up my computer. The light's flashing on my telephone. I know I should check the message, but why? It's probably some reminder of some upcoming "Shopping Queen Extravaganza." Just another opportunity for me to go out and say, *Hi, this is Lili coming to you from some random shopping center. We've got such great deals here, and I'm so happy that I can barely contain myself.* I roll my eyes and shake my head. Out of the corner of my eye, I see Anna.

"Aren't you going to check that?"

"I wasn't planning on it."

"I don't know why you want to get fired." She ducks back behind the cubicle wall.

I don't. I mean, not really. I just get tired of plastering a smile on my face and acting like I care about the sales of clothes or furniture. The welcome screen on my computer comes up, and I'm prompted to enter my password. After pressing a few short keys, I'm in. The home screen comes up, and my cursor is an hourglass while programs begin loading. "Uhhhh." I don't have time for this. I look over at the blinking light and give in, picking up the receiver. I push the voicemail button and enter my password. The robotic voice says I have two messages. The first was left last night around five.

"Lili, it's Béla. Hey, I think I might have just caught a big break in the abductions case. I've got a parent of a girl who's missing. They say they have some big information they want to share. I'm meeting them tonight. Anyway, call me tomorrow. I'll let you know what I find out."

He hangs up, and the robotic voice is back, announcing my second message. "Lili, this is Attila. Tomorrow morning, I want you to go to the Piac in Pest by the river. The big one. There's a special something or other going on there. Be there at nine. Take Tibor and get a variety of shots. Pick what might be most popular. Find someone interesting to talk to. Maybe one of the shop owners or something. We'll go live to you at nine-forty-five."

I look down at my watch. It's 9:13 a.m. I jump up, grab my coat and purse, and run to Tibor's cubicle. Luckily, he's there editing some film.

"Come on. We've got to go now."

"Where?" He's concentrating on the screen and not looking at me.

I slap him on the shoulder, and he finally looks at me. I don't want to yell and bring attention to us. Our boss, Attila, thinks we're already there. I show him my watch and whisper. "We're live from the Piac in Pest at nine-forty-five. We've got to go."

He shakes his head and stands, grabbing his jacket and camera. "How long have you known about this?"

"I just heard Attila's message on my phone."

"Really, Lili?"

He glares at me, and we rush out to the news van.

Twenty minutes later, we're pulling up outside the Piac. Before he even comes to a stop, I'm getting out. I've got to go in and scout out a location and see if I can find someone to interview before he parks and finds me. I walk as fast as I can in three-inch heels. The Piac is a big indoor market. It comprises hundreds of small shops. Everything is sold here—food, clothing, art, home décor, you name it. I fly around the ground level, not sure what I'm looking for but hoping to find something that catches my eye. Most of the goods are food. There are several butchers with all kinds of meat and sausage in freezers. Not what interests my viewers. There are produce vendors with every type of paprika imaginable. But Hungarians have seen peppers ad nauseum. I go up to the second floor, and when I reach the midway point, I see it. It's a shop with handstitched tablecloths and runners. But it's the Zsolnay and Herend porcelain dolls and dishes that catch my eye. This is precisely what Atilla wants.

I find the shop proprietor, and after a fair amount of convincing and selling, she agrees to be interviewed on camera. I have no idea how Tibor has found us, and we're set and ready. I look down at my watch. They're going to throw it over to me in one minute. I worry about how my hair looks, and I don't know what I'll ask the sweet lady next to me. In my ear, I hear the news anchor setting me up. She's explaining where I am and talking about the ongoing sale. Tibor points to me, and the camera light comes on.

"That's right, Rea. I'm here at the Fővám tér market in Pest. They're having a massive sale on several beautiful items. I found the cutest little shop on the second level, and I'm lucky enough to have the proprietor, Szilvia, here with me today. Now, Szilvia, you make many of the pieces in your shop, right?"

Just before going on air, I told her to talk to me and not pay any attention to the camera. But, as is usually the case with amateurs, she's looking at the camera exclusively.

"Yes, I make them."

I was hoping for more, but I improvise.

"Ah, they're so beautiful." I point to an elegant white tablecloth. I step closer to her in an effort to get her focus off the camera and onto me. "Did you make this?"

"Yes."

At least she's looking at the tablecloth now.

"Can you tell me a little about it? How long did it take you?"

She looks back at the camera, and I move forward, trying to get her attention on me.

"It took about forty hours."

I whistle and point out the intricate stitching. "And how much are you selling this for?"

She smiles. She's a sweet, little lady who seems terrified by the question. I can see her mind has gone blank. I examine the tablecloth and find a price tag.

"It looks like you've marked it down from nine thousand forints to five thousand. That's an incredible deal." I turn back to the camera. "That's just a sampling of what you can find here, Rea. All kinds of beautiful, handcrafted items at half price or less. People better make sure to get down here before all the best stuff is gone."

I listen as Rea repeats back in my ear, "Wow, Lilli, that's a fantastic deal. I can't wait to go out there myself."

I smile my most dazzling smile and say, "Better get here quick. Items like that tablecloth won't last long."

Rea says she will, and Tibor holds up his finger, indicating our camera is still live. I smile into the camera while listening to Rea.

"We have breaking news. A reporter named Halasz Béla has been reported missing since late last night." Tibor gives me the all-clear signal and swings the camera off his shoulder, but I plug my other ear and listen through my headphone.

"Last night, Béla's wife reported him missing after he didn't come home. This morning, police went to his office at *Magyar Hírlap* and confirmed nobody had seen him since six last night when he left the newsroom. We'll continue to follow this developing story. If you have any information on

Béla's whereabouts, you're encouraged to call the number on the screen below."

Rea stops talking, and they go to a commercial. Tibor walks closer to me.

"Lili? Are you okay?"

I look at him and place my hand on his shoulder to steady myself. My head's spinning, and I feel like I might faint.

Chapter Thirty-One

Peter

Peter walks through Times Square on his way to Forty-Second Street station. It's ten in the morning, and the square isn't as busy as peak times. But still very crowded. Besides the enormous electronic video boards and massive billboards, the square is littered with the usual suspects. Tourists abound, taking pictures and pointing. Street performers approach them trying to make a few bucks. And then there are the celebrity impersonators. One woman with a blond wig and white dress makes eye contact with him. Peter tries to avoid her but is unsuccessful.

"Hi, big boy. Want to take a picture with Marilyn?"

Peter can't help smiling at the forced raspiness in her voice. He looks around, exaggerating an attempted search. "I'd love to. Is she around?"

The woman smirks, puts a hand on her hip, and flips her wrist. "*I'm* Marilyn."

He keeps walking. "I thought you were dead?"

He's past her now, and she calls out to his back, "I came back for you, handsome."

He smiles and keeps walking. He reaches the subway-station entrance and descends the stairs. He's headed north today, toward Uptown and Queens. He looks around the platform scanning the faces of the other soon-to-be riders.

The train comes, and he gets on, standing and holding a strap above him. As always, the car is full. He rides five stops until he reaches Ninety-Sixth Street, then exits. A few other people leave with him, one guy he takes note of. That's the second time he's seen him. He noticed him first when he turned around to talk to Marilyn in Times Square.

He walks up the steps and turns to his right. He's only a few blocks from his destination but doesn't go directly there. Instead, he walks up Second Avenue until he comes across an apartment building with a person coming out. He rushes forward, catching the door before it shuts. He enters the apartment and lingers in the back by the elevators. After less than a minute, the man who's been following walks by. He looks in at the building but doesn't stop. Peter creeps forward to look out the glass doors and watch him. The man crosses the street and finds a spot in the shadows. Peter walks to the back of the building and finds an emergency exit. The sign on the door says a siren will sound if it's opened. He examines it more closely and sees no wiring and no alarm. It could be on the outside, but he doubts it. The sign is a common trick. He takes a breath and pushes the door open. No sound. The door leads to a small alleyway. He exits, turns left, away from his tail, and walks further down Second Avenue. He continues along Ninety-Fourth Street until he reaches First Avenue and heads north again. He looks behind himself one more time but sees no one.

After five minutes, he walks into the front entrance of Metropolitan Hospital. He enters the elevator and exits on the third floor, hoping nothing has changed. He walks to the nurse's station and sees the familiar face he's looking for. She looks up and sees him; her eyebrows shoot up in surprise.

"Peter? Where did you come from?" She stands and moves around the station and hugs him. "What are you doing here? I thought you left and went back to Romania?"

"Hungary."

She puts her hand to her cheek. "Right, Hungary. When did you get back?"

"Only a week or so ago."

"Are you staying?"

"I'm not sure yet. Just kind of playing it by ear."

She steps back, looking him up and down. Carol was Karen's best friend. They worked together for years. "You look good. Better." He nods. The last time she saw him was six months after Karen died. He was obsessed with the case. He wasn't sleeping and was in a horrible place mentally and emotionally. "I'm so glad." She steps forward and hugs him again. "Sorry," she says, patting him on the shoulder. He can see tears in her eyes. "It's just I've worried about you so much. It's so good to see you looking like your old self."

She goes around the nurse's station and sits back in her chair.

"What about you? How are you?" he asks.

"I'm okay. Life is busy. Tommy is playing T-ball and Sarah's in dance. It seems like Trevor and I don't see each other as much. We're either working or running the kids around."

Peter shakes his head. "Take it from me, make time for each other. You don't know what the future holds."

She looks down and taps her pencil on the desk. "It's not the same around here."

He looks away and chews on his lip. This is harder than he thought. It's the first time he's been here since she died. "I know."

"I really miss her. It feels like a part of me is missing when I'm here without her. I can only imagine what you must be going through."

He swallows and looks away. He's got to get it together. This isn't why he came. He's got a purpose.

"Listen, Carol, I need you to walk me through the last day you saw her. We never talked about it. Did anything unusual happen? Her killer is still out there. I can't rest until he's found."

She looks him in the eyes, reading something. Finally, she clears her throat. "Don't you think if there was something I would have told you?"

"I know. But there has to be more. Just tell me everything. Don't leave anything out."

"Okay, hold on. Let me do my rounds real quick, and I'll be back."

She stands and walks away, and he's left leaning against the station listening to machine beeps and telephones ringing. A couple nurses Peter recognizes come by and ask if he needs help. He tells them he doesn't. They don't seem to recognize him. *Do I look that much different?*

Carol comes back and sits down. "Okay, so there is one thing. She left early; did I tell you about that?"

Peter frowns, "No. How early?"

She waves a hand. "Oh, only like fifteen minutes. She said she got a call from you and had to leave."

"Me? She said *me?*"

"Yeah, she said you wanted to meet her. She was really anxious, you know, excited."

"Did she say anything else?"

"No, I covered for her, and she left. As I said, it was only fifteen minutes early, and she was so excited. You were in such a bad place afterward. I thought if I told you, it would just break your heart more. It was so cute. She couldn't wait to see you." She reaches out and puts a hand on his. "You two had something, you know? To be married twenty years and still be so excited to see each other." She shakes her head and smiles at him.

He takes her hand. "Thank you for telling me, Carol. Thank you for being such a great friend to both of us."

Chapter Thirty-Two

Zsuzsa

I exit the bus and pull my coat tighter. It's late afternoon, and the sun is setting behind the Buda hills. Shadows extend from the seemingly endless sea of *lakóteleps*. We Hungarians call the large communist apartment buildings *lakóteleps* or housing estates. *Estate* is a liberal use of the word. During the Russian occupation of the Cold War, communists stole farms and homes from local citizens. They forced them into these block cement buildings requiring them to work in factories. Újpest, the fourth district of Budapest, had several of those factories. That's why so many *lakóteleps* have been built here. Thousands of people live in a geographically small area.

I rarely come to Újpest. In fact, I can't remember the last time I was here. It's on the Pest side of the Danube River. *Új*, in Hungarian, means "new." So, this is supposed to be the new part of Pest. Maybe in 1950, but now, in 2001, it looks crowded and dirty. At least twenty other people get off the bus with me. They all scurry like rats while I stand looking at the paper in my hand, trying to decide which way to go. A man about my age watches me. I can see him out of the corner of my eye. He got off the bus with me but seemingly has nowhere to go. As I stare at the paper, I can see him approaching. *Ugh, what does he want?*

"Need some help?"

I look up and flash him a smile. "Yes, I'm looking for a friend's apartment. But I only have the address and don't know where to go."

He smiles, and his teeth aren't horrible. He's an okay-looking guy. He's tall, about six feet. He has brown hair and hazel eyes. I can tell he smokes by the faint-yellow stain on his teeth and fingers when he takes the paper from me.

"Oh, yeah. It's that building right there." He points to the second building on the right. "I can take you there."

"Really? That would be great. My boyfriend is waiting for me, and I'm already late."

His face falls, and I feel a little bad. I don't want to lie to him, but I also don't need him hitting on me. It would be a waste of his time and mine. I've already got the information I need.

He looks down at his watch. "Oh, sorry. I'm late too. It's just that second building." He points again and heads in the opposite direction.

I turn away and smile. Am I a brat? I kind of am. But why lead him on? When I was younger, I might have. I liked playing with men's emotions. Not now. I'm too mature for that. Ha! Plus, I wasn't interested in making small talk with the guy while he tried to "get to know" me.

I reach the door to the apartment building and look at the names on the buzzer board. There must be sixty different buzzers. It makes sense, six apartments to a floor. I go up on tiptoes and look at the top row. I see the name and think about buzzing but hesitate. What am I going to say? *Hi, your daughter is dead. I'm a complete stranger. Want to talk to me about it?* Behind me, the door opens, and a young guy, mid-twenties, holds the door for me.

"You going in?"

I smile, thank him, and enter. I walk over to the elevators and push the button. After a minute, it rattles to the bottom, and a short, plump woman exits. She doesn't even acknowledge me. I step inside the metal box and press ten. The door rattles closed, and the overhead light blinks. Nothing about this inspires confidence.

The elevator reaches the top floor with a screech and a rattle. I quickly step out, reminding myself to take the stairs down when I leave. On either side of the elevator are metal gates. Each gate has three buzzers corresponding to the number of apartments on either end. I step closer to the gate and squint, looking for the right door. I see it, following the wire to the correct buzzer. I take a deep breath and ring the bell. Nothing happens, and I consider ringing again when the door opens. It's a young girl, maybe nine years old.

"*Szia*. Is your mother home?"

She looks at me with big brown eyes and nods. She walks away, leaving the door open. After a minute, her mother comes out. She looks at me curiously.

"Yes? Can I help you?"

"Yes, hello. My name is Zsuzsa. I knew your daughter, Judit."

The woman peers at me more closely, her eyes narrowed.

"How did you know Judit?"

"Can I come in? I won't take much of your time."

The woman stares at me, then finally comes forward and unlocks the gate. She ushers me into her tiny apartment and suggests we sit at the kitchen table. The kitchen is a mess, with dishes stacked up in the sink. I'm not judging her. I know she's a single mother and has two jobs. She's doing her best to provide for her family. Add to that the murder of her oldest daughter. That's a mountain for anyone.

She sits down at the seat across from me. "So, what's this about?"

"I want to talk to you about Judit."

She pulls out a pack of cigarettes, puts one between her lips, and lights it. After getting it going, she takes a drag and blows it out. "You said that already. What about her? Are you with the police?"

"No, I'm not with the police."

"Then who are you?"

"My name is Zsuzsa, and I read about your Judit. Do you know there are a lot of girls her age going missing in Budapest?"

The woman shakes her head and rubs at her bloodshot eyes. She looks tired. "No, I don't read the papers much or watch the news. I don't have time for it."

"I understand."

"Do you? Do you have kids?"

I'm taken aback by her sudden coldness.

"No...I don't."

"Then you probably don't understand. So don't say that you do."

I raise my hands. "I'm sorry. I didn't mean to offend you. I'm just saying that I can understand that your life isn't easy."

She blows out a stream of smoke. "That's an understatement. Look, until you're a mother and have a teenage daughter, you won't 'understand.' I tried, okay? Judit started hanging around some girls from out of town. Girls older than her. I told her not to, and she didn't listen. Now look what's happened to her."

She looks at me, and her face morphs from fury to sorrow. Tears well up in her eyes. Her cheeks go red, and she sobs. I feel an overwhelming sense of compassion for her. I'm unsure what to do. Should I go to her? After a minute, she gains some control and takes a drag on her cigarette. She shakes her head. "I'm sorry. I'm just so tired."

I sit with my hands in my lap. I wish I could do something for her.

"Ma'am, do you know who killed her?"

She looks at me, and although she doesn't say anything, a message passes between us.

"Will you tell me?"

Again, she looks at me, the cigarette smoking in her hand. Finally, she shakes her head.

"Look, as I said, girls Judit's age are going missing all across Budapest. But here's the thing, Judit's case is different. She's from Budapest. Almost all the other girls are from somewhere else, either foreign or the country. And they just go missing. Judit's case is odd. She was missing for a week before she was reported, and not by you. She was reported by a classmate."

She looks at me, and I know she wants to tell me. I can see it in her eyes. She wants to unburden herself. She starts to speak when her eyes dart to the hallway behind me. I turn and see movement there. Her younger daughter is standing in the hallway listening.

"Magda. Go back and watch TV."

The girl runs away down the hall. When I turn around, her mother is standing.

"You have to leave. Forget about Judit and me. Please don't ever come back."

Chapter Thirty-Three

Detective Szabo

"Detective Szabo, this is Captain Nik Dončić of the Slovenia National Police."

I extend my hand, and he grips it. He's average height, maybe five foot ten. He's muscular with a dark beard, green eyes, and shaved head. Neither of us speaks the other's language, and just like the Interpol officer, we resort to English.

"Nice to meet you, Detective Szabo. Welcome to Slovenia."

He has a deep voice, much deeper than I expected. He's wearing a police-officer uniform—dark-gray trousers with a light-blue button-down shirt. Badges and symbols cover the shoulders and sleeves. He wears a bulletproof vest and a gun strapped to his chest and waist. After leaving Director Toth's office, the director had called and informed the Interpol and Slovenia National Police.

"We've been watching the building for several hours now. There's been absolutely no movement. Nobody in or out."

I nod and look back at the old, seemingly vacant building as he shakes hands with Farkas, Katona, and Arpad. The four of them introduce themselves. We drove in from Budapest today. It didn't take too long, only four hours. This is my first time in Slovenia.

The building is an old rundown factory. It looks like it might have been a tire-manufacturing plant. Since the GPS device came back online, it's been broadcasting from here. It's inside the building, but we can't tell precisely where Officer Kocsis is. Assuming the GPS device is still on her.

My English is poor. It's easier for me to understand than to speak. But I do my best, utilizing hand motions. "We had a situation like this in Ukraine, Kyiv. We break in, and there are six girls. Maybe ten men guarding. They use guns. We must be careful."

Captain Dončić nods, as does Litz, the Interpol officer. He's an Austrian and looks like the stereotypical version of the Aerian race. He's tall, athletic, with blond hair and blue eyes.

"We will go in first; Interpol will be behind us in support. Once we've cleared the building, we will call you in."

I nod and look at Farkas and Katona. They're nodding also. Captain Dončić turns and waves his team to surround him. They're dressed in full combat attire, complete with masks, vests, and guns. He has a building diagram and points and gives instructions in Slovenian. Heads of the twelve officers bob to his instruction. One officer asks what sounds like a question, and Dončić nods and explains. Finally, he turns back to us and gives a thumbs-up. The Slovenian officers spread out and converge on the building. We don't move. From the road, it's easy for us to have eyes on the structure and watch them.

When all the officers are in position with the Interpol officers behind them, Captain Dončić gives the order, and they breach the front door. Blinding heat emanates from the front of the building as a bomb explodes. A concussion of noise comes next. The three officers closest to the front door are blasted through the air and deposited at least fifteen feet from the building. We four Hungarians duck and cover our heads as small pieces of shrapnel fly onto the street. One of the officers shoots into the open structure, and Dončić waves his hands and yells. The officer stops but keeps his gun trained on what used to be the front door. The Interpol officers move forward while the Slovenian officers fall back and attend to their fallen colleagues.

Cautiously, the Interpol agents enter the building and, within five minutes, give the all-clear signal. No shots were fired in the building. Seems like it was empty. It's been secured without incident. If Kocsis isn't inside, maybe we can at least recover the GPS device. I move forward and wave for the other three to join me. As we draw near the building, I look down and see one of the fallen Slovenian officers. His vest and trousers are torn, and he appears to be missing his right arm. Blood covers the ground all around him. His colleagues are applying a tourniquet while he screams and thrashes. Another, to my right, is a female police officer. She's covered in blood and soot. She appears unresponsive.

Officer Litz meets us at the front of the building and instructs us to follow him. I can't tell if it's the poor lighting or something has changed. His face is grim and seems to have lost some of the color it had before. We follow him through a hallway to a large room. The smell is a mix of dust and smoke. It's empty, other than a large metal table in the center. I squint to see better, then gasp and look away. Before turning back, I take a deep breath and muster the courage. I look again. On the table is a naked body. It's gray and ashen, void of color. It's obviously female. As we grow closer, I force myself to look at the face, knowing I'll recognize it but not wanting to believe it. Yes, I know the face. I feel as if I've been kicked in the gut. It's Officer Kocsis, the undercover agent we placed to be abducted in the club. Beneath her chin, at her neck, is an extensive black line of dried blood. Her throat's been savagely cut.

Officer Litz looks at us grimly and points to her fingers. Several of her fingernails are missing having been pulled out from the ends. She's been tortured. I feel lightheaded, and the room begins to spin. I lean over and put my hands on my knees, sucking in big breaths. Finally, once I think I've recovered enough to stand, I look at Litz.

"Do you know her?"

I nod. "Where is GPS?"

He shakes his head, and I look over at Arpad, our IT specialist. He has his laptop with him, and it's open. He shows me a map on the screen. It indicates we're standing on the blinking red dot. I turn back to Officer Kocsis and examine her. Looking at her face, I notice one cheek bulging, almost like something is pressing against it. Hesitantly, I reach out and push it with my finger. I can feel something hard under the skin. It's unnatural. I extend my finger and insert it into her mouth between her lips. I curl the finger and feel something hard, but it's not her teeth. It's metal or plastic. I pull my finger out and reach back inside with two fingers. I pinch the plastic piece and pull it out. It's the GPS device.

I hold it up, and the group of us examine it. I look at my team, and I know they're thinking the same thing I am. This is a message. The kidnappers wanted us to find it and see her brutal murder. Without saying it, they've broadcast their message: Do this again, and more will die.

Chapter Thirty-Four

Peter

Peter sits at the dining room table, enjoying the family dinner with Gary, Becky, and Rachel. Becky, a marvelous cook, prepared salmon with asparagus, salad, and wild rice. It's the second time she's made it since he's been living with them, and it was just as good or better this time. Gary pushes back from the table, a glass of white wine in his hand.

"I don't know how you do it, Becks, but I think you continue to get better every time."

She smiles and pats him on the arm. "Thanks, honey."

Gary turns and looks at Peter. "Would you believe it? Before we got married, I never ate like this. It was all pasta and cheese."

Peter chuckles. "I would believe it. I knew your mother."

Gary laughs. "True. Mamma never made anything healthy. It was all dishes that ended with an *a*." He lovingly smacks his wife on the arm. "Would it be so bad for us to occasionally have some old-fashioned Italian food? Would it kill us?"

Becky looks at him and, with a straight face, says, "Yes." After seeing the surprise in her husband's face, she explains. "Maybe not right away. But I want to keep you alive as long as I can. I like your paycheck."

Gary roars with laughter and stands and kisses her before taking his plate to the sink and washing it.

"Uncle Peter?"

Peter turns and looks at his niece.

"I got my grade back from my report on Hungary."

"Oh yeah? How'd you do?"

Rachel beams back at him. "I got an A. The teacher even said it was the best report in the class. She said she learned new things about Hungary from it. Thanks for helping me with it."

"You're welcome, sweetheart. It was fun for me too."

She stands and kisses him on the top of the head, then takes her plate to the sink and washes it. Gary slips out and heads to his office while Rachel goes down the hall to her room. Only Peter and Becky remain at the table.

Becky holds her wine glass and peers at him. She's always had a way of making him feel like she's looking into his soul.

"What?" Peter asks.

"How are you?"

"I'm great."

"No, I don't want that answer. I want the truth."

Peter chuckles and shakes his head. "Becky, what do you want me to say? I'm good."

"You've been back in New York a few weeks now. What have you been up to?"

Peter worries he's misread the conversation. Is she hinting that he needs to get his own place? "I've been visiting old friends. It's been good to see them. But look, I'll start putting some effort into finding my own place. I really appreciate you and Gary and your hospitality."

She glares at him. "You think I'm asking because I want you to move out? I thought you were a detective. That you could read people. I'm asking because I want to know what you're up to. What you're working on. I know you. And I know you're back to looking for Karen's killer. Just tell me the truth."

Peter looks away and lays his hands flat on the table. He picks up his right hand and begins tracing the outline of his left with his index finger. "When I was in Hungary, I got into a trafficking case. I was following a man who was abducting young women and exporting them to Croatia. Except, I didn't know that's what it was. I thought it was a simple infidelity case. Anyway, the guy almost killed me and killed himself in the process. From that case, I got a job offer with the National Police in their trafficking task force. While working with them, I learned there was a mole in the police force. It was something I wasn't expecting, and that person put me in jail to try and hide the truth. Anyway, it changed my perspective on everything. I viewed Karen's case from a new vantage point. I realized she was killed to get to me. The cops I was working with here were involved in something and were afraid I'd expose it. By killing Karen, they got me to stop investigating. They got rid of me without killing me."

"And now you're trying to expose them?"

Peter nods.

"Sounds dangerous."

"It is."

"Do they know?"

"What? That I'm investigating them?"

"Yeah."

"My former partner, Tony Caruso, confronted me the other day. He threatened me."

She sighs. "Peter, what are you doing? They killed Karen. Don't you think they could kill you too?"

"I can't let them get away with it, Becky. I can't."

"But last time, they didn't kill you. They killed someone close to you to get to you."

It's the first time Peter thinks about this, but he dismisses it.

"They followed me today. They won't stop until they get me."

She stands from the table and picks up her plate. "Peter, I know you don't care about your life, but we do. And don't put us in any danger, especially Rachel."

He stands, picks up his plate, and comes around the table to her. "Becky, I have no intention of putting you in danger. It's me they want. If anything happens to me, go to the FBI. Tell them about Tony Caruso. Tell them he's been stealing drugs from the evidence locker. Make them investigate it. Okay?"

She sets the plates in the sink, then comes back and hugs him. "Oh, Peter. Don't let them hurt you. Go to the FBI right now. Tell them what you just told me."

"I can't. Not yet. I need one more piece of evidence. Without it, it'll never stick, and they'll skate."

Chapter Thirty-Five

Director Toth

I check my electric-blue tie and navy-blue suit one more time in the full-length mirror in my office. My wife says this bright-blue tie brings out my eyes. I don't know about that, but I care about how I look on TV, and she's a better judge of fashion than I am. I exit my office and walk past my secretary's desk. We make eye contact, and she mouths, "Good Luck." I shrug and walk down the hall. She's been much better at her job than the last one. That woman only lasted two weeks and wouldn't return to the office after quitting. We had to mail her the final paycheck. I guess I scared her. Twice I found her crying at her desk. The last time, she went to lunch and never came back. All I did was raise my voice a little.

I open the glass door separating our offices from the lobby and hear the buzz of people congregating. Before walking down the stairs, I look out over the crowd. There must be thirty people here, including reporters, cameramen, and photographers. A makeshift podium has been placed in the center of the floor, and the press stands in front of it. Molnar Ferenc, my sister's son, stands at the bottom of the stairs waiting for me. He's an annoying kid, and I avoid him as much as possible. But I promised my sister I'd get him a job, and press correspondent seemed as good as any. Whenever he sees me, he can't decide what to call me. Sometimes he calls me Director, and sometimes he calls me Uncle.

"Director, the podium is all set for you. The press has been informed you will read a brief message and then open up the floor for questions. I'll be here if you need me." *Pssh, what's he going to do? Fumble over his words until they give up and leave?* I thank him and nod. Turning to the podium, I stride over, unfold the prepared speech, and adjust the microphone. A hush falls over the crowd, and I'm aware of camera flashes.

"Thank you for coming. As many of you know, Nagy Béla, a longtime reporter and columnist for the *Magyar Hírlap*, has been missing for over thirty-six hours. Béla was last seen in his office at the *Magyar Hírlap* at 5:00 p.m. the day before last. Like all missing-person cases, our office has given this case the highest priority. If anybody has information about Béla or his whereabouts, we encourage you to call our tip line. Béla is a father and husband, and we at the National Police, along with the Budapest Police, are doing everything we can to find him. I'll now take a few questions."

Fifteen hands shoot up with calls of "Director" and "Director Toth." I point to the pretty blond woman in the bright-blue skirt and jacket. I've never seen her at one of these before.

"Director Toth, do you believe Béla is alive?"

I adjust the microphone, giving me time to articulate a response. "Yes. Our hope is that Béla is alive. Right now, the case is classified as a 'missing person' case. We have no evidence to support anything else at this time."

A tall man in the middle of the pack has kept his hand up the entire time. I make eye contact with him and point while others start calling out to me. "Yes, you in the middle." He's holding a pen and has another behind his ear. He's wearing a jacket and tie, but the tie is loose, hanging several inches from his neck.

"Sir, what do you think happened to Béla? And could it be related to his last couple of articles in the newspaper about missing girls in Budapest?"

I want to roll my eyes, but I keep a solemn expression as I consider the question. "I'm not ready to speculate on what might have happened to

Béla. Our hope is that we can find him safe and sound and return him to his family."

"And what about the articles he wrote? Could this be related?"

I shake my head. "We have no reason to believe an article written about a missing teenage girl in Pápa could relate to a missing forty-five-year-old man in Budapest. It seems highly unlikely. More than unlikely. I'd say more like a one-in-a-million chance."

A brunette woman in the back raises her hand, and I point to her.

"Mr. Toth, why are there so many abductions lately in Budapest? It seems like there are several every week. Many of them are young girls. Is Budapest no longer safe?"

I look over at Ferenc, and we make eye contact. This is my way of telling him no more questions. I look back at the reporter. "Actually, abductions and missing-person cases have not increased in Budapest in the last few years. In some instances, the cases have been more high profile. But the case count has remained steady. In fact, missing-person reports are lower in Hungary than in many of our neighboring countries. Moreover, murders, thefts, and all manner of violent crimes have dropped significantly over the last few years. Budapest has never been safer. I want to thank the thousands of officers and agents in both the National Police and respective cities throughout Hungary for their tireless effort to stop crime. We should all be thankful for their service."

I look at Ferenc again, but he doesn't move. I swear a hamster is running on a wheel inside his head. I turn back to the raised hands and voices and cut them off myself.

"Thank you for coming. As we learn more, we'll be sure to send out press releases."

I walk off the podium and glare at Ferenc.

Twenty minutes later, I'm sitting at my desk, my suit jacket hanging from the rack on my door, my sleeves rolled up to my elbows. My tie now resembles that of the reporter in the middle of the pack. My hands are steepled, and I stare in front of me. A knock at the door rouses me from my thoughts.

"Come in."

The door opens, and Rákosi Gyula, head of the Major Crimes Unit, stands looking at me. I motion him in, and he closes the door and takes a seat across from me.

"What do you have?"

He looks down at the file in his hands, then back up at me. The man has some of the thickest glasses I've ever seen. I wonder if they cost triple the amount of a standard set.

"Not much, yet. As you know, lately, he seemed to be fixated on missing-person cases. Especially those involving teenage girls. We obtained a copy of the most recent one from his editor." He looks down at the top sheet in the file. "Nothing groundbreaking. Some speculation about what's happening with these girls. Nothing we haven't seen or thought before."

I nod and turn in my chair so I can look out the window.

"There was an interesting note in a notepad on his desk."

My head whips around, and I stare at him, urging him to go on.

"Seems he had an appointment the night he went missing. We don't know where yet. But he wrote on his notepad, '9 tonight.' We're working to get access to his email. Maybe that will shed some light on this mystery appointment."

I stare at him, waiting to see if he says anything else. When he doesn't, I ask, "How do you know it was that night? Maybe the note was for a different night."

He shifts in his seat. "We know because of the placement of the note. The chronology matches. It was among other notes from the day."

I purse my lips and scratch my ear. "Anything else?"

He shakes his head, and I dismiss him. After he's shut the door, I pick up the phone and dial the number I know by heart. After one ring, the voice answers.

"We've got a problem," I say.

Chapter Thirty-Six

Lili

After the indoor Piac, Tibor and I had to go to a farmers' market in Kőbánya, then the West End Mall. That's made for plenty of time in the van sitting in traffic. After trying several times to strike up conversations, Tibor finally turned up the radio and left me to my thoughts. I'm anxious to get back to the office and browse the internet to learn more about Béla. He's missing? What happened to him? I don't know him well. I've only talked to him on the phone a couple times and exchanged emails. But he never seemed like an unstable person. Could it be his wife? Isn't it always the spouse who ends up being the murderer? Murder? Why do I think he's been murdered? They only said he's missing. Maybe the stress of his job was too much for him. Perhaps he ran away.

Finally, we've reached the office. I jump out of the van and don't wait for Tibor. He's got to gather up all his camera equipment anyway. I go through the doors, ride up the elevator, and speed walk to my cubicle. For once, Anna isn't sitting in hers. I swear, that girl never gets out. I press the power button after putting down my purse and removing my coat. I sit, nervously drumming my fingers on the desk. Finally, the password prompt comes up, and the home screen appears. I move the mouse around, but, as always, the hourglass icon is up instead of a cursor. I look at my phone. It's blinking again. I don't care. Atilla can fire me. I've got to know what happened to Béla.

The hourglass goes away, and I double-click the browser button. The search engine comes up, but I'm unsure where to go. I type in his name, Nagy Béla. Pages and pages of results come up. It's a prevalent name. I refine my search and type, "Nagy Béla reporter missing." This is much better. I click on the first option, which is actually the newspaper he works for, the *Magyar Hírlap*. I scan through the article looking for any new information. He was last seen at 6:00 p.m., almost forty-eight hours ago now. His wife claims he never came home that night. He said he had to work late. He was seen leaving the office at six by one of his colleagues. The officer in charge of the investigation, Detective Rákosi, is quoted as saying, "We're following all leads at this time. We haven't ruled out anything, including foul play. We have no reason to believe he's anything but alive."

I click out of the article and go back to my search results. I peruse several more articles but don't learn anything new. The police seem to have no idea where he is. Eventually, after I've read everything, I pull up my email. It's quiet in the office. Most of the regular nine-to-five people have gone home, and all that remain are those who will be on air tonight. I've got a couple emails at the top. One is from my boss, Attila, and one is from someone in HR about payroll changes. It's the third email that grabs my attention. It was received two days ago at 5:30 p.m. Why haven't I seen it until now? It's from Béla. I open it. –

Lili,

I left you a message about this. I think I might have caught a big break in the abductions in the city. A parent of a girl who has been missing for nine months reached out to me. They call themself "Concerned Citizen." They say they have information about who took their daughter. I'm going to meet them tonight. They don't want to be on the record, but I think it's a legitimate source. Let's talk tomorrow. Maybe we can work together on something.

Béla

I sit gripping my mouse, my mouth agape. I lean back in my chair but can't take my eyes off the words on the screen. The police are going to want to see this. I might be the only person who knows where Béla was going that night. Well, I don't know where he was going; he didn't tell me that. But I knew who he was going to meet, this Concerned Citizen. What happened? Did someone know they were meeting? Is the Concerned Citizen missing also? Maybe he's missing too, and it hasn't been reported. Or perhaps the police know, and they aren't saying. Or maybe the Concerned Citizen wasn't who he said he was. Perhaps it was a setup.

For the next half hour, I search for information on any other missing male in Budapest. There are several possibilities but nothing concrete. Finally, I shut off my computer and head home. After entering my apartment and fixing myself something to eat, I sit down and watch Duna Television. I see myself at the farmers' market in Kőbánya. Most people wouldn't be able to tell, but I can see how preoccupied I am. After my bubbly, cheery report, there's a press conference from earlier in the day. It's a guy by the name of Director Toth, head of the Hungarian National Police. He talks about Béla's disappearance and other abductions in the city.

Finally, I switch off the TV and go to bed. As I lay there, unable to sleep, I continue thinking about the possibilities. Béla must have been taken by those who are abducting the girls in the city. That means he must have been getting close to exposing it. If they killed him, I could be in danger if I continue. But if I don't, Béla will have been killed for nothing. I've got to keep pushing. In fact, I need to turn up the pressure. This is what I've always dreamed of.

Chapter Thirty-Seven

Peter

Peter leaves early in the morning. So early it's still dark. Though, it is January, after all. The sun doesn't rise until after 7:00 a.m. this time of year. He's arranged to meet his friend Lieutenant Bridges before Bridges has to be at work. Only the glow of streetlights illuminates the streets as he walks to the subway line. After boarding the train, he takes a seat and looks around. The car is surprisingly crowded for this early. Well, is it really that surprising? This is Manhattan, a place full of ambitious people who eat, sleep, and drink work. They're competitive and obsess over getting ahead. Hoping they will someday get that promised promotion. They go to bed and set their alarm clocks for 5 a.m. Then, after thinking about a coworker and how they were assigned a specific project, they turn back to the alarm clock and move up the time to 4:45.

Peter reaches Fulton Street station and exits. Last night, he took a calculated risk. He waited around to talk to Becky. He debated going to Gary but decided against it. He knew if he had gone to Gary and told him what he had learned at Karen's hospital and from Kaminski's widow, Gary would have encouraged Peter to go to the FBI. Heck, Gary might have picked up the phone right then and called himself. By acting like something was troubling him, Peter knew Becky would ask him about it. It's something he's always loved and admired about his sister-in-law. From the first meeting, he could tell how much she cared for other people. She's the type of person who puts others before herself. That's why she and Karen were so close. They were cut from the same cloth.

No doubt, after talking to Peter, she was troubled. She would have confided in Gary but made Gary promise not to tell. Today, Gary would ignore his wife's desire for secrecy and call one of his contacts with the FBI. Soon, the FBI would contact Peter. Maybe they'd even begin tailing him. That's why he needs to meet with Lieutenant Bridges today. If he can get access to the evidence log, he knows he'll be able to prove that drugs have been stolen after being confiscated. And if Bridges doesn't deliver it. He has the last piece of the puzzle.

Peter walks through the Titanic Memorial Park toward the bridge and is reminded of the last time he had a secret meeting on a bridge—with his friend Detective Kovacs on the Margit Bridge in Budapest. He and Kovacs had been investigating the rest of the task force trying to determine who the mole was. They knew someone was feeding the traffickers information. Shortly after meeting in the middle of the bridge, a car jumped the curb and cut Kovacs down at the waist as they compared notes. His body was severed in half as Peter watched him fly off the side of the bridge into the freezing water below. Given how that turned out, was this really the brightest meeting spot? Peter shakes his head. That can't happen again here. There aren't any cars on the bridge. At least where the pedestrian path is.

Peter reaches the staircase at Park Row Brooklyn Bridge Underpass and looks behind him. Curious, he thinks, nobody is following him today. Why would they stop? As he starts up the staircase, he notices a large man descending the stairs opposite him in a dark coat and hat. Peter moves to the side to let the man pass, but as he does, the guy leans toward him and slams him into the staircase wall. Peter doesn't have time to react as he's punched in the stomach. He doubles over as he feels the man club him on the back. He hits his knees. A gun is pressed into his left temple, and the man speaks to him in a whisper.

"Don't make a noise. Stand up, and walk back down the stairs. Get into the van at the bottom."

Peter tries to follow the man's commands but has difficulty standing. The shot to his back knocked the wind out of his lungs. Peter steadies himself against the railing and walks hunched over, back down the stairs. As he reaches the bottom, someone grabs him and pushes him into the back of a seatless van. He slides along the floor and comes to a stop as he hits the opposite side. He groans and rolls over to lie on his back. He looks around the van. Before he can see much, the man who hit him places a dark pillowcase over his head. He hears the van door shut and tires squealing.

Chapter Thirty-Eight

Zsuzsa

I sit listening to the ringing in the receiver. Maybe it'll go to the recording. Five. Six. A voice comes on, and it's so cheery I think it's the message machine.

"Hello, this is Gábor."

I wait, expecting him to carry on with his message. But he doesn't. It catches me off guard. I was totally expecting the recording. "Um," I manage.

"Yes?"

"This is Zsuzsa."

I can hear the surprise in his voice when he answers. "*Szia*, Zsuzsa."

"*Szia*, how are you?" What a dumb question, but I can't think of anything better to say. If I got the machine, I would apologize for the other day in the restaurant. Then I'd thank him for the flowers and ask him to call me back. Now all that seems to have flown out of my mind.

"I'm doing good. Thanks for calling. How are you?"

"I'm doing well. Thank you for the flowers."

"Oh, you got them?"

"I did. They're beautiful."

"I'm glad you like them."

We both sit listening to the other end of the phone, unsure of what to say next.

"Hey, look," I finally say, "I'm sorry for how I was at the restaurant the other night. I got some bad news and wasn't prepared to see you. It wasn't about you. I'm glad you cared enough to come in and see me."

"You don't have to apologize. I should have let you know I was coming. It was rude of me to come unannounced."

"No, it wasn't. You were a customer coming in to have dinner and a drink. There's nothing wrong with that. I didn't handle it well, and I'm sorry."

"Thank you. And it's fine. It's really good to hear your voice. I didn't know if I'd hear from you again."

"It's good to hear your voice also."

"Are you working tonight?"

"I am."

"What time are you off?"

"Pretty late, actually. I have to close up. It'll probably be around ten."

"How about a drink after?"

I look down at my clothes. I'm wearing jeans and a tank top. The tank top has a wine stain on the front. "Uh..."

"Oh, come on. Just a drink and some conversation."

I feel a little flutter in my chest at the prospect of seeing him tonight.

"Okay."

"I'll meet you at your restaurant at ten?"

"Okay."

At 9:55 p.m., he walks through the front door. It's been a few days since I've seen him, and I'm unprepared for how handsome he is. His hair is perfectly groomed. He's clean-shaven, wearing a tight V-neck sweater. It shows off his muscular build. He sees me behind the bar and walks over. The restaurant's empty. I've let all the staff go home.

He looks at me and smiles. "*Szia.*"

"*Szia*," I say back, and I can feel myself blushing. "I was thinking, what if we just stayed here?"

"What do you mean?"

"I mean, last time you were here, I wasn't exactly nice to you. Maybe we can make up for it. I can serve you a drink here, and we can talk."

He shrugs. "You don't mind staying at work?"

"Not at all. It's not really work if I'm not being paid."

He smiles, and I can't help his magnetic pull on me.

"Is that your way of telling me you want a tip?"

He's teasing, but I can't help blushing more.

"I only expect a tip if the service is good."

He chuckles. "Okay, but you'll have a drink with me?"

"Absolutely."

I tell him to take a seat at the bar, then lean over and look into his eyes. They're so beautiful I feel myself melting into them.

"So, what can I get you?"

He smiles, and I can see his eyes drop to my chest for a split second. "How about a whiskey sour?"

"Coming up," I say and turn around to get the whiskey.

While I make it, I look up and see him watching me. After I serve him, I make myself a Manhattan. I slide it to the seat beside him and come around the bar to sit down.

Once I'm seated, we clink glasses and say, "*Egészségedre!*"

After we both take a drink, I play with the straw in my cup while he watches me.

"So, how are things?"

He smiles. "Good."

"I think we're going to take your advice and try that free-drink or appetizer idea."

"Nice. You'll have to tell me how it goes."

I take another sip and watch him out of the corner of my eye. I can smell his cologne. He smells as good as he looks. He seems to be letting me guide the conversation, probably because of how things went last time. He looks a little less confident.

"So, how are things with your ex-wife?" I ask.

He looks at me, and I smile a teasing smile. He laughs and takes a drink of his whiskey.

"Oh, it couldn't be better. All that talk about ex-wives being horrible. It's not true at all."

"Really? Maybe you shouldn't have split up."

He rolls his eyes. "Yeah, right." He rubs his glass with his thumb.

Now I turn my barstool so I'm facing him. "Why did you split up?"

His eyebrows raise, but he doesn't immediately answer. "That's a question that should be easy to answer but isn't."

"How so?"

"What's the longest relationship you've had?"

"A couple years."

He nods. "We were together ten. In the first few years, everything was great. Then we had our oldest, and things got more hectic. We started spending less time together. We were working a lot, and when we weren't, we cared for her. Then our second came along. Before we knew it, we were barely spending time together, and when we were, we were arguing."

"Was it her fault?"

"No, not at all. Well...it was both of us. But I'm as much to blame as anyone. I became grumpy and started seeing all the things she did wrong instead of those she did right. She grew more and more demanding, and we got further and further apart. One day she asked me if I was happy, and I told her I wasn't. She agreed and proposed a divorce." He takes a drink and sets it back down. "I moved out later that week, and we've been separated since." He turns and looks at me now. "It's funny. Now we get along great. We share custody of the kids and hardly argue."

"Would you get back with her?"

He shakes his head and sighs. "I don't think so. It got pretty bad there for a while. I wouldn't ever want to be back in that place again. I'm happy with where we are now."

"I'm sorry you had to go through it."

He shrugs. "It's okay. I learned a lot from it. I think if I'm in a situation like that again, I'll do a lot of things differently." He looks at me more closely. "Can I ask you something?"

I suddenly feel a little on edge, unsure what he'll say. But I agree.

"You said before that you were dating someone else. Did that have anything to do with why you were upset when I came in the other day?"

How does he know that? I can't hold his gaze and turn back to my drink. I pick up the straw and start playing with it again. "Yes. I cared a lot for him. But...he had to leave the country for work and may not return. He's an American Hungarian. He grew up here but lived most of his life in New York City. He came back, and we met and hit it off. But he had to go back and likely won't return."

I'm watching him out of the corner of my eye. He nods and takes a drink.

"There's something I've always wanted to say to you," I say.

He gives me a curious look.

"What do you mean?"

"Something you did when we were kids. Well, I was a kid. You seemed so mature."

He chuckles. "Why does that sound more like an insult than a compliment? I hope you don't think that of me now."

"What? Why?"

He chuckles. "Nothing. What did you want to ask me?"

He looks at me, and I lose track of what I was going to say. I'm lost in his eyes. I look down and play with my straw again.

"You probably don't even remember this. But, one day, your sister and I were riding bikes on the gravel road by the church. We were probably nine or ten. There was a football field at the park across the street."

"I remember that field. It's still there now."

"Right. Anyway, you were playing football, and we were watching you and the other boys as we circled around trying not to look obvious. On one of the turns, the ball was kicked out of the field onto the path in front of me. I tried to avoid it and caught one of my shoelaces in the chain and flipped off the bike. Everybody saw it. I was horrified. I was on the ground with my hands and knees bleeding. I could hear the boys laughing. My hair was long, and it was covering my face, and I was grateful because they couldn't see me cry. I heard footsteps and thought maybe your sister was off her bike and was there to help me. But it was you. You stopped the game and came over to help me. My hands and knees were bleeding, and I didn't think I could ride anymore. You helped me up and brushed the pebbles and dirt out of my cuts and scrapes. You got me to sit on my bike seat, then you pushed me home. Do you remember that?"

I look up into his eyes.

"No," he says and laughs.

"Yes, you do," I say, slapping his shoulder.

He shrugs. "Okay, maybe I do. But that's your question?"

I feel my cheeks color. "No."

"So what's your question?"

I look him in the eye. "Why did you help me?"

He takes a drink. "Because I felt bad for you."

"But why did you feel bad for me?"

"Because you fell."

"Yeah, but none of the other boys helped. They laughed at me. Why did you? Did you know?"

"Know what?"

"Know I had a crush on you. Did she tell you?"

He chuckles. "She didn't have to tell me."

I can feel my cheeks color again as I look back down. "So you did know."

He shrugs. "Yeah, I knew. You were too young for me, but I was flattered. That crash looked like it hurt. I knew you needed help."

"Well, anyway, thank you. It meant a lot to me." I point to his drink. "Do you want another one?" He shakes his head, and I'm grateful. Suddenly I feel tired and want to head home. "Let me just put a couple things away and wash these glasses, and we can head out."

He nods and sits, watching me as I tidy up. I grab my coat and purse from the back office, and he walks with me to the door where I lock up.

"Can I drive you home?" he asks.

"Sure."

We don't say much on the drive, and after five minutes, he pulls up in front of my building. He gets out and opens the door for me, and I walk to the front door and turn around. He's standing close, and I look up into his eyes.

"Zsuzsa, I really like you. I'd like to see you again soon."

"I'd like that too."

He starts to lean forward. I think about stepping back, looking away. But I don't. I do want this. He leans down and presses his lips to mine as I close my eyes. His lips are firm but gentle, and I can feel myself struggle to breathe with excitement.

After just the right amount of time, he steps back, not pushing things further.

"Can I call you tomorrow?"

I nod, not trusting myself enough to speak. He opens the door for me, and I go in. I give a little wave and walk to the elevator. When it comes, I turn around and see he's still watching me. He smiles and waves as I go in.

Chapter Thirty-Nine

Detective Szabo

I reach the Buda side of the river via Margit Bridge and continue east, winding my way through busy, crowded streets. I pass Moszkva tér and eventually turn right onto Hűvösvölgyi Street. This is one of the prettiest streets in Budapest, especially in the fall because of the trees lined on either side. Spring isn't bad either, especially in the week or two when blossoms cover the trees. But late January, with no leaves, it's only average. The street is vast, with two lanes of traffic on either side and the streetcar track running down the middle. Many traffic lights are along the road, and I find myself lost in thought as I drive. Starting and stopping every mile or two.

Last night we got home from Slovenia, and although I was exhausted, I found myself tossing and turning in bed. I couldn't get the image of Officer Kocsis out of my head, lying naked and cold on that table in the abandoned factory building. Her throat was cut, and she had been tortured. Why? What information were they trying to get from her? She knew very little about our operation. She was selected because of her age and looks. What information did they want from her? How did they know she was working with us?

As head of the human-trafficking task force, I'm the one who put her in the position. I thought we could protect her with the GPS device. I was clearly very wrong. The guilt I feel is unbearable. Kovacs put Varga in a similar position but didn't let her be taken. He was right, and I was wrong. He should still be alive and running the task force. At the time, I thought it was cowardice, his decision to protect Varga. Now I realize it was wisdom. That girl's death is on me, and I don't think I'll ever be able to get over it. I thought about going to the director this morning and turning in my badge. The only thing that kept me from doing it was a desire to bring justice to her. I've got to find the traffickers. Even if it costs me my life.

The road turns into Szilágyi Erzsébet Street as I go further into the Buda Hills. The streetcar tracks now run adjacent to the street, and beyond them is a forest of bald trees. In a few weeks, the leaves will make the forest so thick you won't hardly be able to see into them. I sigh and shake my head as I follow the red Volkswagen Passat in front of me. Peter was right about everything. All that he said would happen has. He said there was a mole in the task force, and there must be. I thought it was him. But he's in America again, and things continue to get worse. The traffickers know what we're doing even before we do it.

He also said I needed to check out the girl from Újpest who was taken but not reported missing by her mother. He said she was the key. She was found dead a few days later, and her mother wouldn't talk to me. That's why I'm here. I need to find out more about her.

I pull into the restaurant parking lot, get out of my car, and move into the building. A cute young girl greets me as I walk in.

"Welcome to Szép Ilona's. Is it just one tonight?" I nod, and she asks me to follow her. She shows me to a table, and I sit down while she hands me a menu. She says, "*Jo Étvágyat,*" and walks away. I look around the room but don't see Zsuzsa. I hope she's in. I called before I came, and they said she was the manager on duty tonight. After a few minutes, a young man in a white shirt and black trousers approaches.

"Welcome to Szép Ilona's. What can I get you to drink?"

I haven't even looked at the menu or drinks. "I'll take a beer."

"Very good. What kind?"

I wave my hand. "I don't care. Any kind is fine."

"Sounds good. I'll be right back."

He leaves, and I see Zsuzsa coming down the hallway behind him. Our eyes lock, and she comes over. She looks good. She's the type of woman a man like me can only admire from afar. I'd never have a chance to score someone like her. Every move she makes is sexy. From the first time I saw her, I was jealous of Peter. That jealousy is back in full force.

"Detective, what brings you to this side of town?"

I eye her up and down as she stands with her hand on her hip. "I heard the food is pretty good. I was also hoping to talk to you for a minute."

She gives me a steely gaze. "I'll talk to Ernő and take over your table. Do you know what you want to eat?"

I look down at the menu and pick out the first picture I see. "How about the *paprikás csirke*?"

"Sounds good."

I give her my menu and watch her walk away, admiring the view. Ernő returns, places a beer in front of me, and tells me Zsuzsa will be taking care of me for the rest of the evening. I thank him, and he moves away.

For the next fifteen minutes, I sit, drinking my beer and watching the other people in the restaurant. Zsuzsa comes out and talks to some of her staff. Finally, she goes back into the kitchen and comes back out with my food. She places it in front of me with utensils and sits down in the chair opposite me.

"So, what did you want to talk about?"

I unfold my napkin and pick up the fork, keeping my voice low. "Did you go out to Újpest and talk to that mother?"

"I did."

"What did you find out?"

"Not much, unfortunately. She's afraid to talk. Someone put a scare into her. I think she's being threatened."

"Why do you say that?"

I take a bite of the chicken over the noodles, and the flavor explodes in my mouth. I can't believe how good it is.

"I almost had her. I could tell she wanted to tell me, but her daughter was eavesdropping. When she caught her, a switch was flipped. She closed down and told me to leave."

"You think it was about the daughter?"

"I do."

"What about her?"

Zsuzsa shakes her head as I continue to shovel food into my mouth.

"No, not about the older one. The dead one. I think it was about the younger one." She leans forward and whispers. "I think she was protecting the daughter she has left. I'm betting someone threatened that if she says anything, the younger daughter will be killed too."

I lean back and wipe my face with the napkin. "Do you think you could get her to talk to you again?"

She shakes her head. "I doubt it. She was adamant I leave."

"Will you try? Maybe wear a wire this time?"

She glares at me. "What, so your mole can listen and kill her? No thanks. I'm not putting her in danger."

I feel a flash of irritation. But she's right. Against my nature, I open up. "Look, I don't know where else to go. I've got no other leads. If I can't get her to talk, the girls will keep disappearing. I need your help."

She peers at me, watching me more closely now. "Why are you so sure you need her to talk? Peter told you, didn't he?" I don't say anything. "I want to hear you say it."

"Say what?"

"You know what. I want you to say Peter was right. That you shouldn't have arrested him."

I take a drink of beer, and she starts to stand. I put it down and grab her hand.

"Okay, Peter was right. I shouldn't have arrested him. He was right about everything."

She looks at me sideways, but I can tell she's starting to soften. She's pretty intimidating. How can a woman half my size scare me like she does?

"And you won't tell anyone else? It'll be our secret?"

I reach up and put my hand over my chest. "I swear."

She sits back and sighs. "I'll try again. But if anything happens to the mother or the girl, I'll hold you responsible. Got it?"

I nod. But the threat is unnecessary. I'd take my own life if anything happened to either of them.

Chapter Forty

Peter

Peter's disoriented. After getting in the van, they put a black pillowcase over his head and handcuffed his wrists behind his back. His insides are on fire, and he thinks one of his ribs might be broken. He can't take a deep breath without a sharp pain crippling him. He has to keep his breathing shallow. Pain shoots through his side and back whenever he relaxes, even for a second, and forgets. He would guess they've been driving thirty minutes. From what he can sense from the vehicle speed, he figures they've either gone across the river into Jersey or into Queens. If he had to guess, he'd pick Queens. They're more likely to have a property to hold him in there. Or worse, somewhere they can stash his body after they kill him.

The van comes to a bumping stop, and he feels his arm grabbed.

"Keep your mouth shut and follow my commands. I don't want to have to shoot you."

It's Tony's voice. He'd know it anywhere. Two other people are in the van. Not that he would know by hearing them. They haven't spoken since he arrived. He knows it because two different men have handled him, leaving another to drive. That's three total. There's Tony, the man who beat him up, and someone driving. He's got a pretty good idea who the driver is.

They pull him from the van, one guy on each side. His head is spinning from the beating he took at the bridge, and the black pillowcase over his face isn't helping. He shuffles his feet as he walks, trying to get a sense of the terrain. He's taking it slow, hoping to buy as much time as possible. It's concrete. Maybe asphalt, although it feels too smooth. Maybe a driveway? As he moves forward, he senses a change. They had been on a slight incline, and now the surface is level. Sound bounces around where before it didn't. They're in some sort of building, but it must not have insulation. The temperature hasn't changed. A shed? Maybe a barn?

They force him to sit. The chair feels metal. Cold. There's no recline to it, and the top of the back hits him low. Probably a folding chair. The handcuffs dig into his wrists as he leans back in the seat. To his surprise, he hears a motor and a spinning sound above him. It's an automatic garage door closing. What light there was from the outside is now gone. Peter sits in absolute blackness. He can hear the three men whispering several paces away, but he can't make out what they're saying. Finally, one walks closer and rips the pillowcase off his head. He blinks against the dim lighting. Inside the room are Tony, the man who beat him on the stairs, and his friend Lieutenant Bridges. Bridges stands over him. He's the one who ripped off the pillowcase.

"You should have stayed away, Peter. When you went to Hungary, it was the best-case scenario. None of us want to do this to you. Not to a fellow cop."

The other two nod. Just as Peter had suspected, Bridges was the ringleader.

"But you had to keep pushing. And what good has it done you? You got your wife killed, and now you're next."

Bridges motions to Tony, and Tony steps forward, a knife in his hand.

"You see, Peter, it's really very sad. After being unable to determine who killed your wife, you decided to take your own life. You slit your wrists and bled to death. You just couldn't live with the shame."

Tony steps behind him, pushes him forward, then raises his arms. He forces Peter to rest his handcuffed wrists on the back of the chair. Peter senses he's preparing to cut his wrists. He's got to come up with something. Otherwise, he'll be dead.

"You'll never get away with this," he says to Bridges.

Bridges laughs. "That's the best you've got? I thought you'd try to negotiate. Maybe beg and plead for mercy. But this?" He clicks his tongue. "Pretty disappointing, Peter."

"I said it because I know something you don't."

Bridges looks at Tony and holds up a hand. "What's that?"

"I'm not the only one who knows."

"Knows what, exactly, Peter?"

"Knows that you guys were stealing drugs taken from busts, then replacing it in the evidence locker with fake stuff. What'd you use? Cornstarch? Baby powder?"

The three of them laugh, then Bridges says, "Peter, you always were too smart for your own good. I hated that in training. I hated being compared to you. We knew you'd figure it out. That's why poor Karen had to die. We were friends. We didn't want to kill a fellow cop. We knew if we killed her, we'd get rid of you. It would have worked, too, if you'd just stayed away like a good boy."

"Now you're going to kill me."

"Well, we have to. We can't have you going around causing more problems. Plus, we gave you a chance to get away. You don't get another."

"What about Kaminski? He was a cop. Your loyalty didn't run deep with him."

Bridges shakes his head. "We didn't want to kill him either. But he was soft. He got scared when you wouldn't let it go and kept investigating him. After he killed Karen, he became too much of a liability. We couldn't trust him. We weren't sure who he might talk to."

"Pretty clever move, you going to his widow pretending to be the chief."

He laughs. "Oh, you liked that? She never even questioned it. She was happy to take the money and keep her mouth shut. That's until you showed up again. It's really too bad. I've always liked you, Peter." He comes forward and hunches over to look into Peter's eyes. "So, how'd you know about the evidence locker? How'd you know about the cornstarch? We've checked, and you've not been there since you started investigating Kaminski. Who are you working with? Who else knows?"

Peter smiles at him.

Bridges looks at Tony, and a message passes between them. Tony walks away and opens the door to the backyard. A couple minutes later, he returns with the end of a hose and a large plastic bin. Tony tells the other guy to go in the back and turn on the water. Peter watches as Tony begins filling the large plastic bin. Once it's mostly full, he calls out, and the guy shuts off the water. Tony throws the hose to the side, and the other guy comes back in. He and Tony go on either side of Peter while Bridges steps back. They force Peter to his knees in front of the water bin. Bridges stands on the other side, looking down on Peter.

"Peter, I'm going to give you a chance to die easily. Tell us who else you've been working with, and we'll slit your wrists and let you die quickly." He crosses his arms. "Hold out, and we'll just see how long it takes for you to talk. But I promise, you'll die in the end. And one of the options will be much quicker."

Peter fights the panic as he looks at the bin of water. At that moment, if he were working with someone else, he might actually give up the name. But there isn't someone. He figured it out on his own. His only chance is to hold on as long as he can and pray for a miracle. He looks up at Bridges. His calm face masks the fear and panic he's feeling inside.

Bridges looks at the two men on either side of Peter and nods.

They each grab one of Peter's arms and, with the other hand, the back of his head. They force his head underwater. Peter fights to stay calm as he holds his breath. He closes his eyes, knowing panic won't help. After maybe twenty seconds, they bring him up, water streaming down his face. He takes a deep breath, but his head is back underwater before he can finish. Again, he fights to control his emotions, but the panic is more real now. This is worse than he could have ever imagined. He considers taking a breath under the water and just letting himself go. But then, an image of Zsuzsa comes into his mind. He thinks about the first time he met her, in the restaurant. He remembers the stroganoff and her teasing smile. Her soft, sweet eyes. He wants to see them again. The thought distracts him just enough to get through until they bring him up.

With water streaming down his face, he looks at Bridges.

"Ready to tell us, Peter?"

Peter takes painful deep breaths. He turns his head and says, "Tony, we were partners. How could you do this?"

Tony looks away. Bridges glares and yells to the two men, "Dunk him!"

Again, Peter's head is underwater. The same cycle is repeated two more times. On the fourth, he can feel the oxygen in his lungs dissipating. His extremities are growing weaker. After probably the same twenty seconds, they bring him up, but before his head clears the water, they force him back down. He never takes a breath. He knows he can't hold on. The urge to take a breath is too great. Just as he's about to give in and succumb, he feels the hands release from his shoulders and head. He springs up, splashing water violently as he falls back to the ground, sucking in huge gulps of air.

The sound of a gunshot reverberates. Peter opens his eyes to see the unknown man fall to the ground. Tony is holding a pistol in his hand, extended toward Bridges.

"Tony? What are you doing?" Bridges yells.

"This has gone too far, Carl. I'm not going to let you kill him."

Bridges reaches for a gun at his belt.

"Don't!" Tony yells. "I'll shoot."

Bridges brings the gun up as Tony fires. Peter's head feels like it might explode from the loud concussion. Bridges falls back, dropping his gun. His face white with shock. He reaches his hand to his stomach and pulls it away. The hand is crimson. Bridges, when seeing his own blood, cries out. He reaches down for the gun now laying on the floor at his feet. Just then, the back door and interior door to the house fly open. People with blue jackets and yellow lettering stream into the garage. Tony, seeing it's the FBI, drops his gun and holds his hands overhead. Bridges is leaning over, gun in hand. Seeing Tony is no longer armed, he swings his gun forward and fires. Tony takes the bullet, slamming him backward.

The garage seems to shake with the blast of gunshots. Multiple FBI agents open fire on Bridges. Bridges takes several shots to the chest and back, then falls to the floor, his gun clattering to the ground. Peter lies on his back, coughing and wheezing but manages to get to his knees. He scrambles toward Tony, arms still pinned behind his back. An FBI officer steps in front of him aiming a gun at his head.

"Stay right there," the female officer instructs.

Exhaustion overtakes him, and Peter collapses. The agent holsters her gun and leans down cradling his head. Agents rush past them toward Tony.

"Peter, I'm Agent Carmichael of the FBI. Can you hear me?"

He looks at her, and if not for the water covering his face, she might see the tears in his eyes. He lies there staring at her, fighting for the strength to speak.

"You should have come earlier," he croaks.

Chapter Forty-One

Peter

Peter sits on the concrete floor of the garage, his legs sprawled out in front of him, leaning against the cement wall. He's wet, cold, and beaten. But none of that matters. He's alive. The FBI agent found him a towel, and he's used it on his head and face. He can still taste the water in the back of his throat. It feels like he has it in his lungs. Never before had he ever believed water had a taste. Then again, never before had he been waterboarded. He came within seconds of drowning.

As he rests, breathing as deeply as his broken rib will allow, he looks at the three men who tortured him. Tony appears to be alive, but his gunshot wound is serious. He's unconscious now, and paramedics are strapping him into a gurney. Bridges and the unknown man lay motionless on the ground, a pool of blood surrounding them. Peter had watched as FBI agents checked their pulses and shook their heads.

He realizes this is a moment he's dreamed of for over a year. Yet, it doesn't feel as satisfying as he thought it would. These three men murdered his wife and, thereby, ruined his life. But his contempt for their actions doesn't match the feelings he harbors for them personally. Tony had been his partner and friend. He knows his family and his wife. Same for Lieutenant Bridges. He knows his wife and daughters. He regrets the pain this will cause their families. It's not that he regrets exposing them. They had to be revealed. They must pay for their crime. But the trail of heartache caused by their actions is far from over. He feels a swell of empathy for their wives and children.

After a couple minutes, Agent Carmichael returns and sits next to him on the dirty concrete floor, a pen and notepad in her hands. She looks at him with concern.

"Peter, how are you doing? Do we need to get you to the hospital?"

He shakes his head, aware of the pain in his side from the broken rib but unwilling to tell her about it.

"Well, we'll need you to go eventually, just to be sure. But if you feel up to it now, I'd like to ask you a few questions."

He nods.

"How'd you get here?"

Slowly, being sure not to trigger another sharp pain in his side, he tells her about the meeting he set on the Brooklyn Bridge. He tells her about walking up the stairs and being attacked. About how he was forced into the van and the pillowcase pulled over his head. "Where are we anyway? Queens?"

Her eyebrows shoot up in surprise. "How'd you know that?"

He shrugs. "Tony's from here. I knew they'd take me to a place they knew well and wouldn't worry about people hearing us. People often revert to places they're familiar with."

She looks at him for a long time before writing anything down. After making a few notes, she says, "You believe they killed your wife; how did you know that?"

"You know my background?"

"I know you were a detective with the NYPD. I know your wife was murdered, and you retired and looked for her killer, then went over to someplace in Europe, then came back."

"Right. While working in Hungary, I got a job offer that led me to be a consultant with the Hungarian National Police. I worked on the human-trafficking task force and learned a mole was in the force, feeding the traffickers information." Peter shrugs and looks away. "It changed my whole perspective on my wife's case. I started to wonder if it was my coworkers. The more I thought about it, the more I became convinced that's precisely what happened. It's funny; the things you notice change when your perspective changes. I remembered odd behavior in the past that meant nothing to me then. With a new perspective, they meant everything. So, I came back here to prove it. The last case I worked before my wife died was a cop whose gun had been used in a shooting. That cop claimed the weapon had been stolen from him, and he was given a slap on the wrist." He shakes his head. "It didn't make sense. I started investigating and found he was involved in drugs. I was closing in on exposing him when my wife was killed. They killed her, knowing what it would do to me. They were right. I quit the force and fell into a deep depression. It took going to Hungary to help clear my mind and bring clarity to the situation."

"So why did they take you now? Why were they going to kill you? You must have evidence on them."

Peter smiles. "I don't. I knew it was them. But I didn't have much on them. I gambled."

"How so?"

"I went to my old precinct, knowing I'd be able to talk with Tony, my old partner. I asked him a few questions, and his answers left me suspicious. I hoped they'd also make him nervous. He told me that cop, the one I was investigating, had committed suicide. I knew I needed to talk to his wife. When I did, she told me Chief of Special Operations O'Hare and Detective Caruso visited her after his death. They gave her fifty grand in cash, claiming it was life-insurance money. That's obviously BS considering no life insurance is paid out in cash. The names of the men were interesting to me. Based on her descriptions, I knew it was Detective Caruso. But the description didn't match Chief O'Hare. Someone was posing as him. The physical description matched Lieutenant Bridges. Then I applied a little pressure, and Caruso took the bait and confronted me. At that point, I knew I was on the right path."

"But all you had was what the widow told you."

"Exactly. But then my wife's best friend told me about how someone had called my wife, pretending to be me on the day she died. My wife believed it and left work early, thinking she was going to meet me."

"So, who was that?"

"Detective Tony Caruso."

"How do you know?"

"Because Tony has always been fantastic at mimicking voices. He can do anyone—Eddie Murphy, Sean Connery, John Madden, President Bush. So I knew he could do me. He was my partner for four years."

"So, he called your wife, claiming to be you, and got her to meet some-where?"

"Yep, but I don't think he killed her."

She looks at him with surprise. "No? Who then?"

"Officer Frank Kaminski. He was their dirty man. Just like the guy here today was the one who beat me up on the stairs. They had him do it. That's why they killed him later. They were covering their tracks and got a new dirt man."

Peter winces in pain, and she sees it.

"Are you sure you're okay?"

"Yeah, I'm fine."

She shakes her head. "Sounds like we don't have a lot of evidence to convict them."

"Actually, you do. I just didn't have it. You know how I said they were selling drugs?"

"Yeah."

"That's your evidence. Go check the evidence locker in the precinct. Investigate the records. You'll find plenty of inconsistencies and missing drugs."

She smiles and nods.

"I do have a question for you, though," Peter says.

"Sure."

"How did you know I was here?"

"Your brother-in-law called the Bureau last night. He talked to some of the top brass. We were trailing you this morning. It was only one person, and he was ordered to wait for backup before entering. Sorry it took so long."

Peter chuckles. "Well, I'm glad the backup came. I would have appreciated it being earlier. But at least they came."

She looks down at her notepad and stands. "I think that's it for now. We'll want to talk to you again, but I think you should go to the hospital and get checked out."

Peter nods and struggles to his feet. The agent motions to someone else, and they open the garage door. He and the agent walk out to the front of the house when a black Audi pulls up. Peter recognizes the car. Gary and Becky jump out and come for him. They embrace.

"Thank you for calling," Peter says to Gary, wincing. He turns to Becky. "And thank you for making him."

She looks at him and grins. "Last night, you knew I would, didn't you?"

He looks at her and winks. Becky frowns while Gary roars with laughter. Peter lets the paramedic assist him into the back of the ambulance.

Chapter Forty-Two

Director Toth

My phone buzzes, and I pick up the receiver.

"Director?"

"Yes?"

"We were able to access the email. You'll want to hear this."

"Come to my office, Gyula."

I hang up the phone and walk to the floor-to-ceiling window behind me. I look down at the bustling city. Cars and pedestrians heading in all different directions. This is the call I've been waiting for, and I can't help feeling anxious. A knock on the door brings my head around.

"Come," I command.

Rákosi Gyula, head of the Major Crimes Unit, walks in, a file in his hand. I motion for him to sit while I take my usual seat. He holds the file closed, waiting for me to tell him to proceed. I extend my hand, and he opens the file.

"As I told you on the phone, we were able to access the email. Most of it was pretty mundane. Correspondence with people at work, other media members, etcetera. Nothing to get too excited about. Then, a few days before he went missing, things changed. A person going by the name of Concerned Citizen emailed him." Gyula pushes the email printout across the desk. I pick it up and read the email I wrote. "As you can see, they claim to be the parent of a missing girl." Gyula takes another sheet from his file and slides it across the desk. "They converse back and forth, and the person wants to meet Béla in person. They ask to meet him on Margit Island the night he goes missing. This person was likely the last person to see Béla."

I look up from the paper and stare at Gyula. "You think they killed him?"

Gyula shrugs. "We don't know if he's dead. We still don't have a body. But something happened there."

"What makes you so sure?"

He takes another paper from his file and slides it across the desk. I pick it up and look at it. It's a photo of small rocks and dirt. I look back at him.

"That picture was taken this morning near the location they were supposed to meet. After some analysis, we determined that something was dragged into the water a few days ago. It's rained since, so we can't determine much else. No footprints remain." He takes out another sheet of paper, another photo. It's a footprint. The print is smaller than I would expect. "That footprint has been left since it rained. Judging from the size, it's either a larger child or a female print."

"Hmm..." I lean back in my chair and exhale. "So what? It's next to a park, based on the email exchange. Aren't there several footprints in the area? Many are probably child size."

He nods and leans back. "Yes, there are. But only one set in that area of the beach since the rain. All the other footprints are near the child's play toy and the other side of the beach."

I reach up and rub my chin. "So, what are you saying?"

"I'm saying, I think someone went in the last day or so. They must have known we'd be coming and covered their tracks."

"You think it was this 'Concerned Citizen?' Don't you think they're likely a male? You say these footprints are from a female or a child?"

"Yeah, that's a tough one. Maybe it's unrelated. Or maybe this 'Concerned Citizen' isn't who they claim to be. Maybe not male at all. Maybe a jilted lover? Maybe someone who wanted Béla dead for some reason. Regardless, we can't even prove he's dead at this point. With nothing else, we're kinda stuck. That's why I'd like your permission to bring divers in. See if anything shows up in the river."

I don't even hesitate. I'm not concerned. "Do it. It looks like this was the last place he was known to be. Let's get whatever we can."

He nods and stands, moving toward the door.

"Gyula?"

He turns back around.

"Can you track this email account?"

He shakes his head. "No, it was a generic dummy account. Anyone could have set it up."

I feel a sense of relief wash over me until he raises his index finger.

"But we can track the IP address the emails were sent from. It'll take a day or two, but we're working on it. I'm confident we can track the computer down. With that, we might be able to find the location of the sender. Who knows, maybe it was an internet café, and someone will remember him or her. Maybe a video camera is in the place."

"Very good. Let me know how the river dive goes."

He gives me a mock salute and walks out, shutting the door behind him.

I sit, reclined in my chair. This isn't good. I pick up my phone and dial the number. Like always, my call is answered almost immediately.

"Yes?"

"I've got something else I need you to do."

Chapter Forty-Three

Lili

After talking with the store manager, I walk out to the shop entrance. Tibor is there, his camera on his shoulder. He's been filming in the mall, getting some B-roll to splice into the report. We'll be live now, but tonight the recording will air to help fill hours of overnight content.

"I just talked with the manager. I don't think it's going to work," I tell him.

Today we're in the middle of Buda at a famous shopping mall called the Mammut. New Yorker, a popular clothing chain for teen women, paid advertising dollars to the station in exchange for a live report from the store. Attila, the station director, told us to come and interview the store manager. I'm supposed to ask her about their 50 percent-off deals and talk about all the "cute" blouses and jeans. I don't want to interview her. I've got something else in mind. I just need to get Tibor to go along.

"Why?" he asks.

Tibor likes my "Shopping Queen" live remotes even less than I do. He's convinced Attila assigned him to be with me as a punishment. Out of the corner of my eye, I see who I've been waiting for. I asked her to come, thinking now would be our chance.

"She's dull," I whisper. "If we interview her, the whole thing will fall flat." I look to my left and pretend to have a lightning bolt of an idea.

"Wait a second," I say and walk over to where Agnes stands. I smile at her but say nothing until I'm close enough for only her to hear. "Thanks for coming. In order to get you on TV today, we're going to have to mix in some clothing talk. Would you be okay with that?"

A worried look crosses her face. "Uh..."

"Don't worry. Basically, we're just going to dress you up in some clothes and ask you how you feel and what you like about them." I wink and put an arm around her. "If you're lucky, I might even be able to convince them to let you take the clothes home."

I walk her over to Tibor, and as we draw close, I say to him, "This is Agnes. I think she'd be perfect for this shot. She's exactly the right demographic for the store."

He looks her up and down, then shrugs. "Whatever you say, Lili."

That was easier than I thought. I take her by the hand and pull her into the store with me. "Let's go get you outfitted." I walk her over to the store manager and introduce them, then say to the store manager, "I thought it would be perfect to interview a girl who might be a shopper for the store. Your demographic watching TV is going to love it. What do you think?"

I know she's not going to argue with me. What does she know about what does and doesn't work on TV? I've done similar things to this before. The key is projecting confidence. She looks uncertain, so I say in my most excited voice, "Oh, this is going to be *so* cute! Your store is going to be flooded with teenage girls. I'm so excited."

That does the trick. The manager brightens and agrees. I feel a little bad. But I remind myself what good television this is going to make. It'll be broadcast way more frequently than a simple remote commercial. Plus, what I'm doing is more important. I brush aside my conscience.

"Can we pick out some clothes for her?" I ask the manager.

"Sure, whatever you want."

I take Agnes by the hand, pull blouses and jeans off racks, and give them to her. She collects them all, then heads into the dressing room. The manager and I stand around waiting as she comes out to model each set. Finally, after the fourth grouping, we agree. I march Agnes over to stand in front of the prominent New Yorker sign in the middle of the store.

"Here's what we're going to do. I'll start the shot by talking a little about the store and the sale they have going. Then I'm going to walk over to you. You don't need to do anything. Just stand there and wait for me. Tibor will be filming the whole time, but I want you focused on me. Just act like the camera isn't even there. I'll ask you a couple questions about how you feel about those clothes and why you like the store. Then I'll ask for some background on you. We'll be live, and that's when we can learn about you and what you've been through. Okay?"

She agrees, and I walk over to a spot where the 50 percent-off sign is visible. Tibor and I discuss a couple things about the shot, and I hear them announce sixty seconds in my ear. I stand in front of the camera, smile, and think about what I'm doing. Can I really go through with this?

After another ten seconds, the anchor says, "Well, today we're all in for a treat. Especially if you have any teenage girls in your life. Lili, our resident 'Shopping Queen,' is out at the Mammut Shopping Center. Lili, I understand you're at a fun new store for teenage girls. Is that right?"

"That's right, Rea. I'm here at the cutest new store called New Yorker." I pick up a royal-blue blouse and hold it for the camera. "Look at this gorgeous blouse. I saw this, and I knew I just had to have it. If you look behind me, there are all kinds of adorable blouses and jeans on sale for fifty percent off. So, if you need some new clothes, or you just want to be the object of every other girl's envy, make sure you come on out here."

I walk across the floor to where Agnes is standing, and Tibor follows me.

"While I was looking around wishing I could own all the clothes in the store, I ran across this girl, Agnes. How are you today, Agnes?"

She smiles, waves, and shoots a quick glance at the camera before focusing back on me.

"Those clothes you have on, I love them. Did you get them here at this store?"

She smiles and does a little curtsey. I love it. "Yep, I picked them out right before meeting you."

I ooh and aww over them and her. "I love them. You look so good. I bet you won't be able to go anywhere wearing those new clothes without being noticed by everyone."

She laughs and smiles.

"So, tell me, Agnes, why do you like this store? Are you from Budapest?"

She shakes her head. "No, I'm from a little town in the country."

I act surprised. "Really? What brought you to Budapest?"

"My friend and I always wanted to live in the big city. After graduation, we decided to come here. She's in school, and I work."

I nod and get a serious look on my face. "And I understand you had a scary experience since you've been here. Is that right?"

She frowns and glances at the camera, but I move toward her to get her focus back on me.

"Yes, my friend was abducted from a nightclub here in Pest. A couple days later, some guy showed up at our apartment and tried to kidnap me also."

I look at the camera to make sure Tibor is still rolling. The red light is on, but he's giving me a curious look. At least he doesn't seem mad.

"Wow, that's terrible. How did you escape from him?"

"I hit him, then found a knife in the kitchen and cut him with it. He ran away."

I shake my head. "That's horrible. I'm so glad you got away. What about your friend?"

"We were so lucky with her too. She was able to escape her captors. But the other three girls that were with her didn't get away. Nobody knows where they are now."

I shake my head and give her a hug, then step back.

"Thank you for telling us your story, Agnes. We're so thankful you're okay." I turn back and look into the camera. "Girls, please be careful out there. These kinds of stories are happening every day. Be careful and be safe."

The red light goes out, and Tibor swings the camera down from his shoulder and looks at me. Our eyes lock. The store manager comes forward and hugs Agnes telling her how lucky she is and how brave. Agnes is beaming when I come over and hug her. It couldn't have gone better.

"You did great." I turn to the manager. "Do you think maybe she could keep the clothes?"

Being put on the spot, I know the manager can't do anything but agree. Agnes thanks her and says she needs to get to work and leaves. Tibor and I walk out, and once we're away from the store, he says without looking at me, "What are you doing?"

"What?"

"Don't give me that naïve act. You know what you did. I hope you didn't get me fired for this."

Chapter Forty-Four

Peter

Peter walks through the entrance at Metropolitan Hospital and sees the white information desk. An elderly woman is sitting behind it and beams at him as he approaches.

"Hi, sir. How can I help you today?"

Peter's very familiar with the hospital, but he isn't sure where he's going.

"Hi. I'm looking for Tony Caruso's room. Can you tell me where I could find him?"

"Absolutely. One sec."

She looks down and scrolls through a sheet on a clipboard.

"Caruso, you say?"

"Yes."

"He's on the fourth floor, room four-fourteen."

"Great! Thank you."

Peter turns toward the elevator, but she calls out to him.

"Now, hun, you won't be able to walk on that floor. There's a locked door. Once you come off the elevator, there'll be a buzzer. Make sure you press that, and let them know who you are and where you're going."

Peter smiles and thanks her. After riding the elevator to the fourth floor he rings the buzzer.

"Yes?" a voice in the speaker asks.

"Hi, my name is Peter Andrassy. I'm here to see Tony Caruso. Agent Carmichael told me I could come."

There's a pause on the other end of the speaker, then the door buzzes.

"Agent Carmichael will meet you at the door. Come in."

Peter steps inside and waits. After a couple minutes, Agent Carmichael comes around the corner and extends a hand to Peter.

"I can only give you a few minutes with him."

"I understand. Thanks for allowing me to come and see him."

They walk down the hall and the agent stops outside of 414 and looks at Peter.

"I'll knock on the door when you need to wrap it up. I can only allow fifteen minutes."

Peter touches her arm. "Thank you." He pushes the door open and steps inside. Tony is lying in the bed wearing a hospital gown. His right shoulder is bandaged, and he has an IV. Peter notices his leg is handcuffed to the bed frame. He's awake and watching him.

"Hey," Peter says.

"Hey."

Peter walks to the left side of the bed. The hospital room is empty, void of any balloons or get-well signs.

"How's your shoulder?"

Tony turns his head to look at it. "It's been better. The shot tore up some ligaments. They say I'm lucky though. I'll live."

Peter nods. Tony turns back, and they stare at each other. Peter isn't sure how to start. He's not even sure what he wants to say.

"Look...the other day, you didn't have to do what you did. Thank you for that."

Tony nods. "It should have never happened."

Peter says, "I came for two reasons. No, actually three. I wanted to thank you, I wanted to see how you're doing, and I want some answers."

Tony closes his eyes and exhales. "Shoot."

"Why Karen?"

"You may not believe this, but it was never supposed to happen. She was never supposed to die."

"Explain it to me."

"It was Bridges's idea. He lied to me. He told me to call Karen and pretend to be you. He said to get Karen to believe she was meeting you at that Italian joint you two like so much. Bridges would be there waiting. He'd talk to her and convince her to tell you to back off. He was just supposed to threaten her."

Peter clenches and unclenches his jaw.

"I had no idea they were going to kill her. I swear. Later that night Bridges calls me and tells me things went bad. Karen wouldn't listen and tried to leave. Kaminski dragged her into an alley and killed her."

Peter feels the tears brimming and walks away, staring out the window.

"Peter, believe me, if I'd known they were going to do that, I would have never made that call."

Peter feels a flash of anger and turns back to him.

"Yeah, well...that's a little hard to believe right now. We were partners, and you were dealing drugs. You never told me. I trusted you. I loved you like a brother."

"I know," Tony whispers.

"Why? Why did you do it? What possessed you to get into that?"

Tony sighs. "One day I'm talking to Bridges. Letting off steam. Complaining about kids, wife, you know how we do sometimes. He tells me to just wait until they get to college age. He starts griping about lack of pay and how he won't be able to send his kids to college. Then he tells me he has an idea. We take a small amount of coke from the evidence locker each week, something small that nobody will notice. He says he knows another cop who will sell it." Tony shrugs. "I think he's kidding, putting me on. I laugh, but he doesn't. He tells me to think about it. He'd cut me in for some of the profit, and I can save the money for my kids. He says I won't even have to do anything but deliver it to the other cop. Before I know it, we're doing it every week. Bridges takes it and replaces it with cornstarch, I deliver it to Kaminski, and Kaminski sells it. It goes along that way for a few months until something happens with a deal. Kaminski loses his temper and shoots a guy. Suddenly, we're covering up the murder." Tony rubs his forehead. "Bridges tells Kaminski to get rid of his gun and claim it was stolen. The idiot does a bad job, and the gun is found. Ballistics match the murder to his gun. Internal Affairs starts investigating, and Bridges gets them to believe the stolen gun bit, and Kaminski gets off with a warning. I figure we're in the clear. Then you start sniffing around. Once that happens, we knew it was just a matter of time. That's when Bridges said he was going to talk to your wife."

A knock on the door pulls Peter's gaze from Tony. Agent Carmichael holds up five fingers and mouths "five minutes." Peter nods and looks back at Tony.

"Who killed Kaminski?"

Tony looks away. "I did."

"Why?"

He rubs his face again. "He became too much of a liability. After killing Karen, he was sure you were never going to stop. He wanted to run. We couldn't have it. We needed you to believe Karen was killed by someone you locked up. Someone who wanted revenge on you. If Kaminski ran, you'd know something was going on. Killing him and making it look like suicide was the best way." Tony shakes his head. "The thing is, you were so destroyed by Karen's death, I don't think we had to do anything. You stopped looking into Kaminski. You left the force. The best day was when we learned you were going back to Hungary."

"Then I came back."

Tony shakes his head. "Then you came back. My heart nearly stopped when you came into the precinct. I knew you'd figure it out, and Bridges was going to kill you."

"That's why you came and threatened me at my brother-in-law's place?"

"Yeah. I wanted to warn you. I didn't want this to happen. But you wouldn't listen. After you talked to Bridges, he started saying we had to kill you."

Agent Carmichael opens the door.

"Sorry, Peter. You have to go now."

Peter steps away from the bed, but Tony grabs his arm.

"Peter, I never meant for any of this to happen. I would have never let them kill Karen; you have to believe that."

Peter stares into his eyes. As Tony talked, Peter felt a range of emotions. Hate. Anger. A longing for revenge. But now, as he stares at him, he also feels guilt. He was Tony's partner and mentor. He should have seen it before, been better. Maybe they could have avoided all this. He looks around the cold room and realizes Tony has nothing left. He's going to prison for a long time, and he's lost his family.

Tony stares at him, longing for him to say something.

Finally, Peter responds.

"I believe you, Tony. I'll never be over what happened to Karen, but I forgive you for your part in it. Thanks for what you did the other day. I appreciate you telling me what happened to Karen. Good luck."

Chapter Forty-Five

Director Toth

I open my eyes and look to the other side of the bed. Eszter has already left and gone to work. Judging by the faint light filtering through the window shade, it's still dark. I roll out of bed, reach inside the closet, grab my robe, and slide on my slippers. I shuffle down the hall and sit on the couch. I look at the clock on the wall. It's 7:16 a.m. I was out late on business and didn't see Eszter or Ildiko yesterday. Both were asleep when I came home. I'm surprised I don't hear Ildiko. She should be up already for school. Eh, I don't care. I'm not in any rush to fight the battle of waking her up and getting her ready, then driving her.

I sit staring at the fireplace mantle across the room. Several family pictures litter the shelf, including the photo of our son when he graduated from the academy and became an officer. It's been three years now. He's been gone three years. In some ways, it feels like longer. I don't want to think about that, and I reach for the remote.

I turn on the TV and start flipping around the channels. Eszter hates it when I do this. She always says I change the channel just as she gets interested in something. At this time of morning, there's nothing on. Several channels are blank, and the others are shopping networks or German stations. There are a few early morning news and talk shows. All feature women who act perky and excited to be awake. Ugh.

Right before I give up and turn off the TV, I run across Duna Television, Hungary's twenty-four-hour news station. I don't typically watch the news. Most of it is opinionated and built for entertainment rather than to inform. But instead of turning off the TV, I watch it, which shows how badly I'm looking for a distraction.

There's a report on our national football team. They've hired a new club manager. There's an international report about an American submarine that accidentally struck and sunk a Japanese training vessel. Nine of the Japanese crew members were killed, along with four high school students onboard.

The following report is back in Hungary. It's here in Budapest, and it's live. A beautiful blonde, whom they call the "Shopping Queen," is at the Mammut. I've been there several times. She's the perkiest of all. She's talking about a clothing store with teenage-girl clothes on sale. I'm tempted to flip the channel, but I enjoy watching her. She's gorgeous. She walks over and talks to a girl who's supposedly shopping in the store, but it's clearly staged. What teenage girl is out shopping for clothes at seven in the morning? The store wouldn't even be open yet. The girl looks familiar. Somehow, I know her. But I can't place how. Then it hits me. She's the girl whose friend was recovered in Ukraine. I turn up the volume to hear what she's saying.

When the report is over and the channel goes to commercial, I walk to my office and shut the door. I pick up the phone and dial the number.

"Good morning, Boss."

"Good morning. Did you see the report on Duna Television just now?"

"No."

"It was the girl who escaped in Ukraine. Her friend just told her story on live TV."

There's a hesitation on the other end of the line.

"What would you like me to do?"

"I've had enough of those girls. They've caused more than their share of problems. Eliminate them."

"Are you sure? You don't want to just abduct them? We might be able to get quite a bit for them."

"No. Get rid of them."

"What about the reporter?"

I picture her again in my mind.

"Let's abduct her. When you do, I want to see her before she gets shipped off. I have some questions for her. But get the girls first. I want them gone before they can do any other media appearances."

"We'll do it today."

"What about Peter? Is he still in New York?"

"He is."

"And the bartender? Have we learned anything from her yet?"

"Not yet."

I bite my upper lip as I think.

"We need to turn up the pressure. I want to know if Peter's told her anything."

I go to hang up the phone, but they stop me. "Hey, Boss?"

"Yeah."

"There's something else you need to know."

"What?"

"You aren't going to like it."

"What is it?"

"There's something else about the bartender."

I'm losing patience. "Yeah, what about her?"

"She's been talking to Detective Szabo. He went and saw her."

This catches me off guard. "Really? What do they have?"

"I'm not sure yet."

I grit my teeth and hiss into the phone.

"After the girls and the reporter, she's next. Keep her quiet."

"What about Szabo?"

"That idiot can fumble around in the dark as long as he likes. She's got twice the brains he has. She's the threat. Find out what she knows."

Chapter Forty-Six

Zsuzsa

I arrived early at the restaurant this morning. Earlier than I needed to. Most of the time, Kata manages the day shift while I take the night. But she called yesterday asking if I could come in today, and she'd take the night. I was excited. I like the change of pace, and it also leaves me with a free night. I called Gábor, and he asked me to dinner.

I'm not used to being here so early, and it's too quiet. I flip on the TV as I take chairs off tables and restock the condiments. I have at least a half hour before any employees arrive. I've never been one to watch the news. I find it depressing and often irrelevant to my life. But ever since meeting Peter and learning about the trafficking in the city, I find myself paying more attention. I keep hoping to see something about the abductions. Maybe if people start paying attention, something will change.

I look up from rolling the utensils as I hear the news anchor, a brunette woman with lots of makeup and perfectly quaffed hair, say something about a missing newspaper reporter. I reach over and pick up the remote to turn up the volume.

"Yesterday, Director Toth of the Hungarian National Police gave a press conference in which he addressed the disappearance of Nagy Béla."

The screen cuts to a mid-fifties gentleman with a bald head and impeccable posture. He's a handsome man in a dark suit and blue tie. As he speaks, something about him is familiar. I think I've seen him before, but I can't place it. Maybe I saw him in the jail when I went to see Peter. Or perhaps the other time I talked to Szabo. The screen cuts back to the anchorwoman, who says, "If you have any information about Nagy Béla, you're encouraged to call the number at the bottom of the screen."

Her demeanor brightens, almost like she is flipping a switch, and she says, "Now it's time for another 'Shopping Queen Extravaganza.' Lili is in Budapest today, and I understand she's out at the Mammut Shopping Center. Is that right, Lili?"

This beautiful blond woman in her early twenties comes on the screen. She's wearing a floral print top and jeans. She's got bright-red lips and a gorgeous smile. She seems to love her job, although I wonder if it might be an act. Nobody can be that perky. I've never seen her before, but from what I can gather, she goes around from place to place, talking about sales and deals and experiencing different shopping excursions. Today she's at a teenage girls' clothing store talking about a sale they're having. She walks over and begins talking with a teenage girl she found in the store. This girl looks familiar too. What's going on here? I've never watched TV and recognized a single person. Now it's happened twice in a matter of minutes.

When she starts talking, I know where I've seen her before. She was one of the girls from Ukraine. I'm just not sure which one she is. The Shopping Queen asks her questions about her clothes, and it looks like a routine sales pitch until it isn't anymore. The conversation turns, and they begin talking about her experience with the abduction. Well, I should say, her friend's abduction and her near abduction. A lump swells in my gut. Does this girl know the danger she's put herself in? Does this reporter care about her and her friend? A great sense of foreboding settles over me.

The two women embrace, then the Shopping Queen says, "Thank you for telling us your story, Agnes. We're so thankful you're okay." She turns and faces the camera with a solemn look on her face. "Girls, please be careful out there. These kinds of stories are happening every day. Be careful and be safe."

The TV cuts to commercial, and I walk to the office Kata and I share. I pull up the computer, and after connecting to the internet, I browse for information on Nagy Béla. My hand comes up to my mouth as I read the first article. It's one he wrote just a few days ago. It's about a missing girl from Pápa, a city about an hour from here. She was here for a competition, then disappeared.

I turn away from the computer and look at the wall. My eyes aren't focused on what I'm seeing. My thoughts are on the implications of what I've just learned. I reach inside the desk and pull out my purse. I rummage around until I find the card I'm looking for. I pick up the phone and dial the number on the card. After a few rings, he answers.

"Hello, this is Detective Szabo."

"Detective, this is Zsuzsa."

"Yeah, Zsuzsa, did you get something arranged with the mother yet?"

"No, I've tried calling, but she won't answer. I think I'm going to need to go over there again. But that's not why I'm calling."

"Why are you calling?"

"Did you see the report on Duna Television this morning?"

"No."

"Agnes, the girl who went with Peter to Ukraine, was on this morning. She was interviewed about nearly being abducted and talked about what happened to Renata."

"What? Who interviewed her?"

"It was weird, a woman who calls herself the 'Shopping Queen' on Duna Television. It seems like it was just by happenstance. I'm worried about Agnes and Renata. Do you know about the reporter, Béla, who's also missing?"

He takes a deep breath and sighs. "Yeah, I know about that."

"He was writing articles about missing girls. I just read one. I don't think it's a coincidence that he's missing now."

There's a pause on the other end of the phone before he says, "Neither do I. Look, I have to go to a meeting. Do you think you could go check on those girls if I give you the address? They need to get out of town. They're in danger now."

"I could after I get off work this afternoon."

"Okay, I think that would be good. I've got a hectic day, and I can't make it until tonight. I don't trust telling anyone else about this for now. Here's the address."

I jot it down and agree to call and give him an update after reaching the girls.

I don't leave work as early as I would've liked. We got busy, and Kata got in a little later than usual. It's almost five p.m. before I reach the girls' apartment building and ding for the elevator. I go up to their floor and knock on the door. Nobody answers. There's not a sound inside the apartment. I ring the bell and knock again. Still nothing. After pacing on the landing for a few minutes, I look at my watch and know I need to go. I've got a date with Gábor in a couple hours, and it will take at least forty-five minutes to get home.

When I get back, I call Szabo and tell him there was no answer at their apartment. He tells me he'll go by and check, and we hang up. I strip off my clothes and jump in the shower, knowing I'm running out of time. Gábor is going to be here soon.

Chapter Forty-Seven

Peter

After exiting the subway, Peter walks a half mile to the bus stop; he rides the bus to the Fifth Avenue/West Seventy-Second Street stop and gets off. After entering the park, he walks past the Central Park Information Kiosk then passes Pilgrim Hill. It's been several years since he last came to the park, but nothing seems different. This has been a day he's dreamed of for so long. He knew exactly where he would go after solving the mystery of Karen's murder. He expects it to be liberating, but he also knows it might not provide the relief he has so long been seeking. He's surprised to see a few buds popping up on a scattering of trees. The last week has been warmer than usual, and a few days ago, the groundhog didn't see his shadow. Maybe spring will come early.

Just like the last time he came, hand in hand with Karen, he finds himself holding his breath. He passes the remaining distance and sits down at a bench in the same spot they had been years ago. He's alone this morning. Nobody else is within earshot. As he looks at Bethesda Fountain, he recalls that glorious day eleven years ago.

They had just left the hospital, following their daughter's final follow-up exam. The doctors told them the cancer was in remission. Catherine was officially cancer free. He and Karen sat watching her sleep in her stroller as they cuddled on the bench. It's the happiest Peter can ever remember being. Never had he been so lucky to be alive.

That day a burden had been lifted. The news was a beacon of hope. That's why he wanted to come here. He wants to relive the moment. He wants to share his happy news with her again. After looking around one more time to verify he's still alone, Peter speaks to her.

"As you know, I've been carrying a lot of guilt. I should have listened to you that day. You were scared, and I brushed it aside. Every time I think of that moment, I wish I could go back. I wish I would have stayed in bed with you. I wish I had listened. I love you and miss you. I miss you every day. I'm so sorry for the hurt I caused you." The words catch in his throat, and he struggles to go on. "From the moment I learned what happened to you, I wanted revenge. I wanted to avenge your death. I thought by doing that, somehow, I'd make it up to you. I'd get closure for you and me. But I don't feel like I think I should. Sure, they're dead now, but you're still gone. I'm still alone. There's still a massive hole in my heart. I don't know if you can hear me. I'm not sure if you're there. But I want you to know how sorry I am. I will always love you."

He looks up at the fountain rising a few feet from him. A bird sits on top, looking at him. As his eyes fall back to the base, a shaft of sunlight escapes the cloud cover and bathes him in warmth. The warmth is more potent than he can ever remember feeling from the sun, almost like an embrace. He looks away from the fountain and up at the radiant light. A burden he's been carrying for over a year lifts from his shoulders. Relief washes over him in a way he knows he will never be able to describe.

When he had first met Karen, her smile had a magnetic pull so strong he couldn't imagine being apart from her. She's all he thought about. When they were together, he felt complete. He knew God meant for them to be joined. When she was gone, a hollowness consumed him. In the six months following her death, he sunk further and further into depression.

He dropped so low he considered taking his life. That's when he decided to go back to Hungary. It was his last effort to find closure and move on.

As he sits basking in the sun's warmth, feeling his wife is finally back with him, a memory floods his mind. They were in their Manhattan apartment. They had just finished watching *Sleepless in Seattle* on VHS. Karen had turned to him and asked, "Would you ever marry again if I died?"

He teased her, asking, "Are you trying to tell me something?"

She elbowed him in the ribs. "I'm serious. Would you?"

He fell to the other side of the couch in mock pain. She watched him, glaring down. He sat up and sighed. "I've never thought about it. But, no, I don't think so."

Her big brown eyes looked into his. "Why?"

"Why what?"

She frowned, clearly not in a teasing mood. "Why wouldn't you marry again?"

He shook his head. "I don't want to think about this." He stood from the couch, walked into the kitchen, and filled the teapot with water. She followed him, sitting at the kitchen counter.

"I would want you to marry again."

He stepped away from the stove and stood on the other side of the counter. "Why?"

Her eyes locked with his. "Because I would want you to be happy. And I know you would never be truly happy again if you were alone."

He went to her and took her in his arms. As he stood hugging her, smelling her hair, he said, "Well, I wouldn't."

She pulled back to look into his eyes. "You wouldn't what?"

"I wouldn't want you to remarry."

A smile played on her lips. "And why not?"

"Because I wouldn't want you to be with anyone else. I couldn't stand it."

They laughed, and he kissed her gently at first, then more passionately. Soon the tea was forgotten as they retreated to the bedroom.

As Peter sits, reflecting on that memory, he knows somehow Karen has brought it to his remembrance, that she's telling him something. He knows he has to return to Budapest.

Chapter Forty-Eight

Detective Szabo

Just another thing Peter was right about. When I talked to him after Kovacs had been killed, he told me someone in the task force was working with the traffickers. I thought it was him. He said it wasn't. He was telling the truth. It's someone else, and the list of suspects continues to dwindle. The only possible candidates could be Varga or Farkas. They're the only ones who have been with us the whole time. Katona just recently joined. Nobody else has access. There's a team of four of us, and I can't trust two of them. I don't have many allies left.

I pull up in front of Agnes and Renata's building and get out. I walk in, summon the elevator, and arrive at their floor. Zsuzsa had been here an hour ago, and nobody was home. The girls were probably still at work or school. Now, they should be back. I hope I'm not too late.

I knock on the door and get no answer. I ring the bell and knock louder. Still nothing. Maybe Agnes was smart enough to realize she would be in danger and found Renata, and they skipped town. If that's true, there may be some evidence of that in the apartment. They would have packed some things.

I examine the door and don't see an easy way to get in without busting it down. Maybe they have a hidden key? I look around. No welcome mat. That would be the most obvious place to hide it. Across the hall, a neighbor has a fake potted plant. I go over and examine it. Nope, not there. My eyes rise to the threshold above the door. I reach up and smile. I hold a key in my fingers. I press the key in the lock and turn the handle. I pause. Should I be doing this? It's illegal for me to enter, but they might be in danger. If someone finds out, I'll claim I heard a disturbance inside. I push open the door and enter. It's dark, and I search the wall for a light, finally finding one.

I can't help holding my breath as I look down the hallway and see her. Even from this distance, I can tell who's lying on the floor. I exhale as a wave of desperation and sadness sweeps over me. Agnes lies facedown. I approach and see the pool of blood surrounding her chest and neck. It's a dark-crimson color. She's been dead for hours. Only one eye is visible, staring straight ahead, lifeless.

If she's dead, maybe Renata is too. I walk into their bedroom and scan the beds and closet. Nothing. I enter the bathroom and see no sign of her there either. Hope rises in my chest. She might still be alive. I cross into the kitchen and find it void of anybody. She's not here. She could have been abducted again. Or found leaving school or work. Maybe they killed her and left her body somewhere. I see a phone on the wall in the kitchen and walk over to it. I dial the emergency number and wait until an operator comes on.

"Yes, this is Detective Szabo." I read off my badge number. "I've stumbled upon a murder scene." I give the address of the apartment. "Please send backup immediately." As I hang up the phone, I hear the front door opening. I draw my gun, unsure who it might be. When I look around the corner, I see Renata. All color has left her face. She was holding a grocery sack, which was dropped to the floor. She stands motionless. I holster my gun and come around the corner. She sees me, and her eyes go wide. She springs to the door, flings it open, and rushes out.

"Wait!" I call after her. I run out the door, but she's much smaller and quicker than me. She's to the staircase as I cross the threshold of the door. "I'm the police," I shout. But it doesn't slow her. She's gone down the staircase. I stumble after her, but I need to lose more than just a few pounds, and I can hear the shuffle of her feet getting dimmer. I won't catch her, so I stop at the window of the landing and watch below me at the front doors. A few moments later, I see her running out from the front of the building. She's fast, and I'd never catch her. I make my way down the rest of the stairs and leave the building. I find my car and hurry inside, then peal out in the direction she ran.

Twenty minutes later, I return to the apartment building. Police cars are everywhere, and there's yellow caution tape blocking the entrance. Two uniformed officers are standing guard, preventing people from entering. I walk up to them and show them my badge.

"I'm Detective Szabo. I called this in."

They hold up the tape, and I enter the building. When I reach the girl's floor, Varga, Farkas, and Katona are there, along with a forensics team.

They all look at me, but Varga is the one who speaks. "Where did you go?"

I take a breath to answer but then think better of it. I can't trust these people. I can't tell them Renata came home and then left, and I have no idea where she is now.

"I thought I saw someone fleeing the building. A suspect. I chased them out, got in my car, and drove around, hoping to find them. But lost them."

"What did they look like?" Farkas asks.

I shrug. "I didn't get a good look. They were too far away. Male, probably five foot eight, maybe a hundred and seventy pounds. Wearing a black jacket and hat."

Looking at Varga and Farkas, I can't help my contempt for them. One of them is a trafficker and murderer. Maybe both. I've got to find out who.

Only Katona is clear. From this point on, I know I have to keep a close eye on both of them.

Chapter Forty-Nine

Peter

When Peter walks into Gary and Becky's apartment, he's surprised to see Gary is already home. It's only 4:00 p.m. on a Friday. Gary's sitting at the kitchen table reading the newspaper while Becky is on the couch reading a book. They look up as he enters.

"Where'd you go today?" Gary asks.

Before he can respond, Becky says, "Don't you think you should be taking it easy? You had a pretty big day recently."

A "big day" is a colossal understatement, but it wouldn't do to argue the point. He looks at Gary. "Would you mind if I use your computer for a few minutes?"

Gary tells him he wouldn't and walks him to the study. He logs on to the computer and connects to the internet, then leaves him. Peter smiles. It wasn't that long ago he walked into an internet café in Budapest without the first clue how to search the internet. Now, he wouldn't call himself an expert, but he at least knows how to conduct a few internet searches on his own.

He opens Internet Explorer and brings up Ask Jeeves. In the search field, he types "news reports Hungary." The search gives him a plethora of options. He's been checking this every day since returning to New York, hoping to see Director Toth in handcuffs. He sees Nagy Béla, the *Magyar*

Hírlap reporter, is still missing. His body has yet to be found. As he looks further down the list of results, he sees an image that rattles him. It's a beautiful blond woman interviewing a teenage girl. Peter recognizes the girl. He clicks the link and waits for it to load. He's surprised to see it's a video. He impatiently waits for the video to download, then plays it. As he watches, his concern grows. He knows he needs to get back to Hungary right away. He closes the internet browser and walks out of the study. Peter sits down on the couch next to Becky.

"I'm glad you're both here. I was hoping to talk to you about something."

Becky sets her book down and waves Gary over. He leaves his newspaper on the table and takes the oversized chair. Peter positions himself so he can look at both of them.

"I really appreciate all you two have done for me. If not for both of you, I would have been dead yesterday."

Becky leans over and pats his hand. "We're so grateful it didn't turn out like that. We'd kind of miss you." She winks at him, and he smiles. Peter feels like he's a kid talking to his parents. Like he's asking for permission and knows they're about to say no. He decides there's little point in delaying.

"I need to go back to Hungary."

Becky has a sharp intake of breath, and Gary leans forward.

"Is that wise?" Gary asks, elbows on his knees.

"The last time you were there, you were arrested. You almost got yourself killed yesterday. Don't you think it's about time you paused for a minute? Maybe take a little while to think about what you want to do with the rest of your life?"

"Believe me. I know how crazy this seems. But you have to understand there are people over there I care about also. I can't sit here and relax when I know others I care about are in danger. My conscience would never allow it."

They look at each other, and Gary leans back in his chair.

"You don't need our permission, Peter. You know that. What else is there?"

Peter smiles. The guy isn't in the position he's in because he's dumb. He knows how to read people.

"There's something I could use your help with."

"What?"

"I need to go back. But I need to be incognito. Could you help me get back in the country without my passport being checked?"

Gary takes a big breath and chuckles. "Well, now. That's a pretty big ask."

Peter raises an eyebrow. "I guess it shows how much I think of you."

Gary laughs, and Becky shakes her head.

"I don't like it. I don't think you should do this." She turns to Gary. "Don't help him."

Gary looks at her and raises a hand in a gesture toward Peter. They start talking like he isn't even there. "If I don't help him, he'll sneak into the country another way. And if he does, he's going to get caught. He's like a teenager. You know they'll sneak out of the house at some point, you just don't know when. At least if I help him, he's got a chance of not getting himself arrested again. Or worse."

Becky shakes her head and picks up her book. Peter's surprised when he sees tears spring to her eyes. He slides over on the couch and puts an arm around her.

"I promise you, I'll be careful. I wouldn't go if it wasn't vital."

She looks up at him, and tears spill out from her eyes and run down her cheek. She throws her arms around him, and he gasps in pain.

"Oh, I'm sorry," she says, moving back and placing a hand on his shoulder.

"It's okay. It's only a rib."

Gary stands and comes over to put an arm around his wife.

"How soon do you need to go?"

"As soon as you can swing it."

"I'll make a couple calls."

Chapter Fifty

Zsuzsa

"Okay, Zoltan, time to head out. I want to go home."

He looks up at me with glassy eyes, and I pray he's not going to cause a scene. Once, a couple years ago, Andras tried to get him to leave when he had too much. He took a swing at Andras. He missed. At the time, I was grateful. Now, I wish he'd connected.

He says nothing, and my anxiety builds. I try the sweet, motherly approach, even though I only feel exhaustion and annoyance.

"I'm sure you've had a long day. It's time you get home and get some rest."

I approach him and rub his shoulder. I swear, he's had so much to drink he's sweating liquor. He looks at me with droopy eyes.

"Are you going to be okay?" I ask.

He bobs his head and swings his leg off the barstool. He has a hand on the bar, steadying himself. He begins to rise and nearly topples forward. I grab him by the arm and help him as he stands. He's pretty unsteady on his feet.

"Come on. I'll help you to the door."

He looks at me, his head swaying. He takes a step forward and puts his arm around my shoulders. I'm surprised by the weight of him. He's average height, but he does have a large belly and round features.

We reach the exit, and he stops and leans against the frame while I push open the door. The night is chilly, and the cold air makes him blink several times.

"Thank you, Zsuzsa."

I smile and pat him on the shoulder. "Are you going to be able to make it home?"

He nods, and I see a twinkle in his eye. He leans toward me, puckering his lips. He's so inebriated I easily dodge the kiss. But I can't get out of the way of his hand as he reaches for my breast. He squeezes it as I step back and slap his hand away. He roars with laughter and walks out the door. He's steadier on his feet now.

"I'll see you tomorrow, love."

I glare at him and slam the door, locking it behind me. I'm alone in the restaurant now. It's late, and I'm exhausted. I stayed out a little too long last night with Gábor. We went to dinner and a movie. It was after midnight before I got back to my apartment. We kissed for several minutes when he dropped me off, and I considered inviting him in. But I'm not ready for that yet, and I think he knows it. He doesn't try and push the issue.

I grab my purse, put on my coat, and do one more check around to ensure all the doors are locked and everything is as it should be. Then I slip out the back door and lock it. It's chilly, but the first inklings of spring are starting to show up. There's a different scent in the air. I might be crazy, but I think I can smell blossoms. The thought gives me some energy, and I decide to walk home rather than wait for the bus.

The streets are quiet. The restaurant is in a residential part of town, and after ten, cars are infrequent. All I hear are random dogs barking. Some are closer than others. Earlier today, I tried to call Detective Szabo but only got his answering machine. I left a couple messages without a callback. I'm curious to know what happened with Agnes and Renata. I wonder if he was able to find them. I hope they're okay.

I need to cross the street. I'm only a couple blocks from my apartment building now. I look over my shoulder to make sure no cars are coming; that's when I see it. I should say, that's when I see *him*. I squint to make sure I'm seeing what I think I'm seeing. The man is hidden in shadow, but he's approaching me and quickly closing the distance. It's too dark for me to see his face. He's coming toward me but still twenty or thirty feet away. Something about his build reminds me of the man who walked past me that night I was abducted after I left the club. A rush of adrenaline courses through me, and I turn and start to run. I get to the other side of the street and steal another glance over my shoulder. He's running now too. He's coming after me.

Terror courses through my body, and I give it all I've got. My legs are pumping as I get closer to my apartment building. He's gaining on me. I can hear his steps behind me. I can't afford to look back. I've got to get to my building. I'm only a block away when a man steps out from the shadows in front of me. I stop and scream as the man comes toward me.

"Zsuzsa?"

He's tall, and I can see his lean, muscular build even through the dark.

"Zsuzsa, it's me."

"Gábor?" I run to him, and he wraps me in a huge embrace. I'm breathing hard, sucking in air, trembling.

"Zsuzsa, what's wrong?"

I turn around and look behind us. The shadowy figure is gone. Gábor must have scared him away.

"A man. He was chasing me."

My head rests on his chest, and I look up at him. He's looking behind us. Searching for the man. He wraps his arm around my shoulders. "Come on. Let's get you inside."

We walk to the front of my building, and I give him the key. I'm shaking too much to unlock the door. We ride the elevator up to my floor, and he opens my apartment door. I turn on the lights and crumble into a chair at my kitchen table. He comes over and kneels in front of me, placing his hand on mine.

"Are you okay?"

I look into his eyes and reach forward to hug him. I rest my head on his shoulder. He wraps his arms around me. We stay like this for a few minutes. Tears roll down my cheeks and make his shoulder damp. I finally let go and stand. I walk into the living room and grab a tissue. I dab at my eyes, not wanting to rub off what mascara I have left. My eyes probably resemble a raccoon.

I turn around and look at him. He's sitting in a chair at the table. The cleft in his chin is more prominent now. He seems concerned, and I feel so grateful that he saved me and decide to open up. I walk over and take a seat next to him.

"It might seem crazy that I think someone was following me. But if you knew what I've been through over the last year, you wouldn't think that."

His eyebrows raise in surprise, but he doesn't say anything. I'm unsure where to start, so I might as well start at the beginning.

"You know how I told you I was recently promoted in the restaurant?" He nods. "Well, the ownership of the restaurant changed hands recently. Before, there was another owner. His name was Andras, and he was killed on a train coming back from Croatia."

His head rears back with this news, and he frowns. I tell him all about Andras. I tell him how young girls working in the restaurant would just disappear. About how Andras had threatened me when I asked about it.

Then I tell him about Kata. About how she hired Peter and how Peter followed Andras. How Kata was taken to Croatia and how Peter saved her. How Andras nearly killed Peter on the train and how he ended up killing himself instead. Then I tell him about working undercover in the club. I tell him about being abducted myself. How I woke up in Ukraine tied to a chair and interrogated by Csaba, the club manager. How Peter and Kovacs saved me. Then I tell him about coming home and Kovacs being killed and Peter being arrested.

"Wow," is all he says when I finish. He rubs his forehead and looks up at the ceiling.

I look at him, and when he looks back at me, I try to read his eyes.

"Wow," he says again, shaking his head.

"I know."

"And that's where Peter is now? In jail?"

I shake my head. "No, he's in America. I'm not sure how, but he got out. I guess he knows someone there with a lot of power. He doesn't think he'll ever be able to return."

Gábor nods. "So, why do you think someone was following you tonight?"

"Well, there's more."

"There's more?"

I shake my head. "I know. But there is."

"Well…"

I tell him about what Peter said to me in jail, about the girl in Újpest who went missing and wasn't reported by her family. How Peter told me that she was the key to figuring everything out. I tell him about how I went to see her mother. And about how Agnes was on TV and got interviewed. About how I went to the girls' apartment, and nobody answered. When I finish, he blows out a deep breath.

"Why do you keep doing this?"

"What do you mean?"

"You aren't a cop. Why do you keep putting yourself in danger?"

I don't have a good answer for him and look down. "I always wanted to be a detective when I was younger."

He looks at me sideways. "Yeah, but look at you. You're a nervous wreck. You're being chased by shady men. There's something more to it."

"What?"

"You tell me."

I look back down and tap my nails on the table. "When Andras took those girls, I didn't know what was happening. I just knew they were disappearing. I was scared, and I didn't do anything. I think about a lot of those girls still. I wonder about them. Where they are now. If they're even alive. It eats me up that I stood by and did nothing. I can't do that again."

He nods, and we lock eyes. I can see there's something else he wants to say.

"What?"

He shrugs. "Is that all?"

"What do you mean?"

"There's no other reason?"

"Like what?"

"Like that you're in love with Peter?"

Chapter Fifty-One

Lili

"Thanks for coming, Lili. Have a seat."

I sit down across the desk from him. Another woman sits in the chair next to me. I've seen her around the office but don't know her well. I think she does something with payroll.

Attila stands, walks to the door, and closes it, then sits back in his chair. He extends his open hand toward the woman.

"You know Niki, don't you?"

I nod and smile at her. I was expecting to hear from Attila after my interview with Agnes. But he hasn't said anything. He also hasn't assigned me any new on-air remotes. That's not all that unusual. I've had a few days here and there where I didn't go anywhere. I've just been catching up on paperwork since.

"I'm going to get right to the point. That interview you did with the girl at the Mammut, did you know she would talk about her friend being abducted and her near abduction?"

I swallow and look at him. "You mean, did I plant her in the shot?"

He shakes his head. "No, I already know you did that. I've talked to Tibor. I'm asking, did you know what she would talk about? Did you know she was going to talk about the abductions?"

I look at him, then at Niki. They stare at me, expressionless, waiting for me to respond.

"Yes."

He nods and looks down at the desk. Niki slides back in her chair.

"I'm not going to get into why. Frankly, I don't care. But because of your actions, Duna Television has made the decision to terminate your employment, effective immediately."

I feel my face flush, my mouth agape. I look over at Niki, and her face is still expressionless. Impassive.

"Why?"

He shakes his head and looks at Niki. They stare at each other, then he looks back at me.

"Your interview has put the station at risk of legal action."

I can't keep the shock from registering in my voice. "Legal action? How?"

"I can't say anything more than this. The girl you interviewed, Agnes. She's dead now."

His words hit me like a thunderbolt. Tears spring to my eyes. He's cloudy as I look at him. Niki leans over and offers me a tissue.

I dab at my eyes, and once I trust myself enough to speak, I ask, "What happened?"

He shakes his head. "I really can't say anything else. I'm afraid anything you learn about it will be from the TV and newspapers, just like everyone else."

Niki hands me a termination notice and reviews a few payroll and benefits questions. They stand and shake hands with me, and I walk back to my cubicle. It's the end of the day, and the newsroom is quiet. Only a few scattered people remain. Niki follows me to my desk and hands me a box. I gather my belongings, and we walk out together. I give her my key card, and she wishes me luck while closing the door. I stumble to the elevator, holding the box. I'm doing my best to keep it together. Once inside, I press for ground level and descend.

When I reach the bottom floor, I notice through the glass doors it's now nighttime. It's incredibly dark. Good, I don't want anyone to see my walk of shame anyway. I've been fired. Instead of winning the respect of the news director, I gave him cause to terminate my employment. Not only that, I might have earned the station a lawsuit. Even worse, I might have been the cause of a teen girl being killed. The tears start again as I walk down the sidewalk toward the bus station.

To my right, a white van stops along the curb. Before I know it, a hand reaches over my shoulder and clamps over my mouth. Powerful arms pull me toward the van. I drop the box and stumble forward, trying not to fall. I'm pushed into the van and slide along the seat. The big man climbs in after and shuts the door as the driver accelerates away.

The man beside me is wearing a mask. He yells to the driver in…English. Why are they speaking English? The man behind the wheel accelerates, and it throws me back on the bench seat. Panic rises in my chest. I realize I need to fight and get away. I kick the man beside me, and I'm sure it hurts because I use my heel. He cries out in pain, and I reach for the sliding door opposite him, nearest me. Maybe I can open the door and roll out, except we're going fast now.

Still, I reach for the door, but before I can pull it open, he grabs my arm and pulls me back. His grip is powerful, but I fight him. I swing my other arm to hit him, but he catches it. Now he has both my hands in his. Again, I try to kick him, but I'm not able to get any real force behind it. Now he climbs on top of me and forces me down onto the seat. Panic rises in my chest. Is he going to rape me?

"Stop it. Just listen for a second," he says in flawless Hungarian. The surprise of this stops me. I peer at him more closely. Do I know him? He releases one of my hands and takes off the black ski mask. He's staring down at me. He's handsome. Much older than me, but he's got a salt-and-pepper beard and striking green eyes. He's got my other hand back in his now. He's holding me at the wrists, straddling me. Something about his face eases my anxiety. There's kindness there. He's not someone I should be afraid of.

"Just listen to him for a second," the old guy shouts from behind the wheel, looking back at me. "He might be ugly, but he's honest."

The guy on top of me rolls his eyes and shakes his head.

"My name is Andrassy Peter. I'm a private investigator. That guy," he inclines his head toward the driver, "is Lantos Tamás. We've kidnapped you to save you. You're in great danger."

Also By D.J. Maughan

Chasing the Wicked

Book four in the Vanished Series

Peter's back in Hungary, but now what? The head of the human-trafficking syndicate doesn't know Peter is back, but pressure is mounting and he has a plan.

After solving the mystery of his wife's murder, Peter Andrassy, a native Hungarian and former NYC detective, is back in Budapest. The leader of the trafficking organization is powerful and vindictive and wants him dead. The traffickers are targeting Peter's friends and allies, including the intoxicating Zsuzsa. Peter knows he needs to protect them without revealing his return. How will he save himself and his friends and stop the trafficking?

Buy Chasing the Wicked and learn if Peter can halt the corruption.

Expected release December 2023

About the Author

This is book three in the Vanished series, and by now, you probably know who I am. I'm not going to bore you with the same bio. To have read book three, you must be enjoying the series. Thank you! I appreciate you giving my writing a shot. It means so much to me. Time is our most precious commodity, and I'm honored you would spend yours reading my work.

When I started writing volume one, *Vanished From Budapest*, I had no idea how long it would take, whether I would enjoy it, and if I would write any others. I'm surprised at how addicting it became. I plan to write for many years to come. The characters in this series feel so real to me. Their story has to be told. The series will span five novels. I hope to publish the fourth volume, *Chasing the Wicked*, before the end of 2023. The goal is to complete book five, *Apprehending the Devil*, in the spring of 2024.

Finally, if you feel comfortable, I'd appreciate your endorsement. I'm a relatively unknown author, and I need help from my readers to promote my books. If you know someone who might dig my writing, please recommend them. I'd also love a rating and/or review on Amazon. I hope you enjoy your next read. Now, back to work for me.